Eugene J. Hall

Lyrics of Home-land

Eugene J. Hall

Lyrics of Home-land

ISBN/EAN: 9783744783071

Printed in Europe, USA, Canada, Australia, Japan

Cover: Foto ©Andreas Hilbeck / pixelio.de

More available books at **www.hansebooks.com**

LYRICS OF HOME-LAND

"THERE'S A CHOIR OF HAPPY VOICES IN THE WOODLANDS SWEETLY SINGING;
OUT AMID THE APPLE BLOSSOMS WE CAN HEAR THEM ALL THE DAY
AND WITH GLAD AND JOYOUS MUSIC ALL THE LEAFY BOUGHS ARE RINGING.
GAYLY SING THE SUMMER SONG BIRDS. HOW WE WONDER WHAT THEY SAY."

(Page 99.)

LYRICS OF HOME-LAND.

BY

EUGENE J. HALL.

CHICAGO:
S. C. GRIGGS AND COMPANY.
1882.

TO

IRVING RETTER HALL,

MY MERRY LITTLE SON,

THIS VOLUME IS AFFECTIONATELY INSCRIBED.

IN YOUTH BE PURE, IN MANHOOD STRONG,
BE FOREMOST IN THE FIGHT,
A BITTER FOE TO EVERY WRONG,
A CONSTANT FRIEND TO RIGHT.

BE BRAVE, MY BOY, NOR YIELD, NOR FALL,
AND IT WILL BE MY PRAYER
THAT THE DEAR LORD, WHO LOVES US ALL,
MAY KEEP YOU IN HIS CARE.

PREFACE.

LEAVING the old New England farm-house where I was born, I commenced my career, beyond my native hills, by teaching a district school. During that interesting period of my existence it was my pleasure and privilege to sojourn with many families of whose simplicity and hospitality I still cherish kindly remembrances. I have heard the pattering raindrops and the rattling hail upon the shingles, and have listened to the howling of the winter wind about the great gables and massive chimneys of many old farm-houses. I have slept in the spare bed, behind whose snowy valance the winter's store of butternuts was spread to dry. I have chased the highway cow, have labored through long, sultry days in field and meadow, have hunted and fished amid the vernal mountains, have been one of the social group accustomed to congregate at the village store, and have often sat by the olden time fire-place and heard my share of that small gossip so common in country neighborhoods. I have traveled from town to town, always mingling closely with the people; and I can say, without exaggeration, that, with few exceptions, I have found kindness, benevolence, generosity and good-will wherever I have been; and therefore can affirm, with good reason, that these very excellent qualities are the most prominent characteristics of the average American. To those who have helped and befriended me I desire to publicly express my gratitude, particularly to John M. Retter of Oak Park, Franc B. Wilkie, Judge Mason B. Loomis and

William M. Hoyt, of Chicago, Illinois, who have been true friends to me when friendship was greatly needed.

Yankees, so called, have always been represented, in both literature and the drama, as sharp-featured, ungrammatical boors, talking nasal nonsense and making themselves and their country generally ridiculous. Doubtless they are eccentric and peculiar people, but in intelligence and education are second to few, if any, people on earth. The Yankee dialect is agreeable to the ear, and, in the expression of ideas, is compact and comprehensive. It is only in the most isolated places, if indeed anywhere, that anything approaching the "conventionalized" Yankee could be found.

It has been my purpose to picture with fidelity the better side of American life, manners and scenery. If I have failed in my undertaking, it is because my eyes have deceived me, or that my pen is powerless to portray the peculiarities of nature, the joys and sorrows of the human heart, the sweet faces and the lovely landscapes I have seen. The following poems may lack grace and beauty, but I have faithfully tried to put a truthful touch of honest nature in them all.

Eugene J. Hall

MILLARD AVENUE STATION, CHICAGO, ILL.,
    August 10, 1881.

CONTENTS.

SONGS OF NATURE.

SOCIETY SKETCHES.

ILLUSTRATIONS.

RUSTIC RHYMES.

THE HOUSE ON THE HILL.

INSCRIBED TO MY MOTHER.

FROM the weather-worn house on the brow o' the hill
    We are dwellin' afar, in our manhood, to-day,
But we see the old gables an' hollyhocks still,
    Ez they looked long ago, ere we wandered away;
We can see the tall well-sweep that stan's by the door,
An' the sunshine that gleams on the old oaken floor.

We can hear the sharp creak o' the farm-gate again,
    An' the loud cacklin' hens in the gray barn near by,
With its broad, saggin' floor, with its scaffolds o' grain,
    An' its rafters that once seemed to reach to the sky;
We behold the big beams, an' the "bottomless bay"
Where the farm-boys once joyfully jumped on the hay.

We can hear the low hum o' the hard-workin' bees
    At the'r toil in our father's old orchard once more,
In the broad, tremblin' tops o' the bright-bloomin' trees,
    Ez they busily gather the'r sweet, winter store;
An' the murmurin' brook, the delightful old horn,
An' the cawin' black crows that 're pullin' the corn.

We can see the low hog-pen, jest over the way,
  An' the long, ruined shed by the side o' the road,
Where the sleds in the summer were hidden away,
  Where the wagons an' plows in the winter were stowed;
An' the cider-mill down in the holler below,
  With a long, creakin' sweep fur the old hoss to draw,
Where we larned by the homely old tub long ago
  What a world o' sweet raptur' there wus in a straw;
From the cider-casks there, lyin' loosely around,
More leaked from the bung-holes than dripped on the ground.

We behold the bleak hillsides, still bris'lin' with rocks,
  Where the mountain streams murmured with musical sound,
Where we hunted an' fished, where we chased the red fox
  With lazy old house-dog or loud-bayin' hound;
An' the cold, cheerless woods we delighted to tramp,
  Fur the shy, whirrin' patridge, in snow to our knees,
Where, with neck-yoke an' pails, in the old sugar-camp,
  We gathered the sap from the tall maple trees;
An' the fields where our plows danced a furious jig
  Ez we wearily follered the furrer all day,
Where we stumbled an' bounded o'er boulders so big
  That it took twenty oxen to draw 'em away:
Where we sowed, where we hoed, where we cradled an' mowed,
  Where we scattered the swaths that were heavy with dew,
Where we tumbled, we pitched, an' behind the tall load
  The broken old bull-rake reluctantly drew.
How we grasped the old sheepskin with feelin's o' scorn,
  Ez we straddled the back o' the old sorrel mare,
An' rode up an' down thro' the green rows o' corn,
  Like a pin on a clo's-line, that sways in the air;

"FROM THE WEATHER-WORN HOUSE ON THE BROW O' THE HILL
WE ARE DWELLIN' AFAR, IN OUR MANHOOD, TO-DAY."

We can hear our stern fathers a scoldin' us still,
Ez the careless old creatur' comes down on a hill.

We are far from the home o' our boyhood to-day,
    In the battle o' life we are strugglin' alone;
The weather-worn farm-house hez gone to decay,
    The chimbley hez fallen, its swallers hev flown,
Yet memory brings, on her beautiful wings,
    Her fanciful pictur's again from the past,
An' lovin'ly, fondly, an' tenderly clings
    To pleasur's an' pastimes too lovely to last.
We wander again by the river to-day,
    We sit in the school-room, o'erflowin' with fun,
We whisper, we play, an' we scamper away
    When the lessons are larned an' the spellin' is done.
We see the old cellar where apples were kept,
    The garret where all the old rubbish wus thrown,
The leetle back chamber where snugly we slept,
    The homely old kitchen, the broad hearth o' stone
Where apples were roasted in menny a row,
Where our gran'mothers nodded an' knit long ago.

Our gran'mothers long hev reposed in the tomb,—
    With a strong, healthy race they hev peopled the land,—
They worked with the spindle, they toiled at the loom,
    Nor lazily brought up the'r babies by hand.

The old flint-lock musket, whose awful recoil
    Made menny a Nimrod with agony cry,
Once hung on the chimbley, a part o' the spoil
    Our gallyant old gran'fathers captur'd at "Ti,"—

"AN' RODE UP AN' DOWN THRO' THE GREEN ROWS O' CORN,
LIKE A PIN ON A CLO'S-LINE, THAT SWAYS IN THE AIR."

Brave men were our gran'fathers, sturdy an' strong,
    The kings o' the forest they chopped from the'r lands,
They were stern in the'r virtu's, they hated all wrong,
    An' they fought fur the right with the'r hearts an' the'r hands;
Down, down from the hillsides they swept in the'r might,
    An' up from the hollers they went on the'r way,
To fight an' to fall upon Hubbardton's height,
    To struggle an' CONQUER in Bennin'ton's fray
O! fresh be the'r memory, cherished the sod
    That long hez grown green o'er the'r sacred remains,
An' grateful our hearts to a generous GOD
    Fur the blood an' the spirit that flows in our veins.

Our Allens, our Starks, an' our Warners 're gone,
    But our mountains remain with the'r evergreen crown;
The souls o' our heroes 're yet marchin' on,—
    The structur's they founded SHALL NEVER GO DOWN.

From the weather-worn house on the brow o' the hill
    We are dwellin' afar, in our manhood, to-day;
But we see the old gables an' hollyhocks still,
    Ez they looked when we left 'em to wander away.
But the ones that we loved, in the sweet long-ago,
In the old village churchyard sleep under the snow.

Farewell to the friends o' our bright boyhood days,
    To the beautiful vales once delightful to roam,
To the fathers, the mothers, now gone from our gaze,
    From the weather-worn house to the'r heavenly home,
Where they wait, where they watch, an' will welcome us still,
Ez they waited an' watched in the house on the hill.

THE HIGHWAY COW.

THE best o' bein's will hev the'r cares,
    There's alwus sumpthin' to cross our way,
To worry an' fret. us in our affairs,
    An' sech wus the lot o' old Deacon Day.
He hed his trials: I'll tell you how
He wus tempted an' tried by a highway cow.

The hue o' her hide wus a dusky brown,
    Her body wus lean an' her neck wus slim,
One horn turned up, an' the other down,
    She wus sharp in sight an' wus long in limb,
With a peaked nose, with a stumpy tail,
An' ribs like the hoops on a home-made pail.

Menny a mark did her body bear,—
    She hed been a target fur all things known,—
On menny a scar the dingy hair
    Would grow no more ez it once hed grown.
Menny a pebble, shied an' shot,
Hed left upon her a lastin' spot.

Menny a cudgel an' menny a stone,
    An' menny a brick-bat o' goodly size,
An' menny a 'tater swiftly thrown

7

Hed brought the tears to her tarnal eyes,
Or hed bounded off 'm her bony back
With a noise like the ring o' a rifle-crack.

Menny a day hed she passed in pound,
   Fur slyly helpin' herself to corn,
Menny a cowardly cur an' hound
   Hed been transfixed by her crumpled horn;
Menny a tea-pot an' old tin-pail
Hed the farm-boys tied to her old stump tail.

Old Deacon Day wus a pious man,
   A frugal farmer, upright an' plain,
An' menny a weary mile he ran
   To drive her out o' his growin' grain.
Sharp were the pranks that she used to play
To get her fill an' to get away.

He used to sit on the Sabbath day,
   With his open Bible upon his knee,
Thinkin' o' loved ones far away
   In the Better Land, that he longed to see,
When a distant beller, borne thro' the air,
Would bring him back to this world o' care.

When the Deacon went to his church in town
   She watched an' waited till he went by.
He never passed her without a frown,
   An' an evil gleam in each angry eye;
He would crack his whip an' would holler, "Whay!"
Ez he drove along in his one-hoss shay.

Then at his homestead she loved to call,
  Liftin' his bars with her crumpled horn,
Nimbly scalin' his garden wall,
  Helpin' herself to his standin' corn,
Eatin' his cabbages one by one,
Scamperin' off when her meal wus done.

Of'en the Deacon homeward came,
  Hummin' a hymn, from the house o' prayer,
His good old heart in a trankil frame,
  His soul ez calm ez the evenin' air,
His forehead smooth ez a well-worn plow,
To find in his garden that highway cow.

His human pashuns were quick to rise,
  An' stridin' forth with a savage cry,
With fury blazin' from both his eyes
  Ez lightnin's flash in a summer sky,
Redder an' redder his face would grow,
An' after the creatur' he would go.

Over his garden, round an' round,
  Breakin' his pear an' his apple trees,
Trampin' his melons into the ground,
  Tippin' over his hives o' bees,
Leavin' him angry an' badly stung,
Wishin' the old cow's neck wus wrung.

The mosses grew on the garden wall,
  The years went by, with the'r work an' play,
The boys o' the village grew strong an' tall,

An' the gray-haired farmers dropped away,
One by one, ez the red leaves fall,
But the highway cow outlived 'em all.

The things we hate are the last to fade;
　　Some cares are lengthened to menny years;
The death o' the wicked seems long delayed,
　　But there is a climax to all careers,
An' the highway cow at last wus slain
In runnin' a race with a railway train.

All into pieces at once she went,
　　Jest like savin's banks when they fail,
Out o' the world she wus swiftly sent,—
　　Leetle wus left but her old *stump tail.*
The farmer's gardens an' corn-fields now
Are haunted no more by the highway cow.

FARMER BROWN'S DREAM.

INSCRIBED TO U. S. GRANT.

HANNAH, I hed a dream last night, that the war again hed
come;
I heard the scream o' the merry fife an' the rattlin' o' the drum.
Again our gallyant boys in blue, with the'r glitterin' guns were seen,
An' our company formed in a solid line upon the village green;
While wimmin were there with the'r leetle ones, an' with menny a
tearful eye,
Ez they bid the husbands they loved so well a long an' last good-by.
There were lovers who parted forever there, an' mothers who tried
to pray,
And leetle babies, who clapped the'r hands ez the'r fathers marched
away —
Away from the peaceful village, with a firm an' solem' tread,
An' down to the fields o' glory, where the furrers an' streams were
red —
Away, in the merry spring-time, an' into the bloody fray,
With the buttercups an' daisies a bloomin' beside the way;
With our war-drums wildly rollin', with our voices jined in song,
An' our colors a gaily flyin', ez we proudly passed along.

Then follered the sultry summer, our faces grew dark an' brown
Ez over the dusty highways we tramped from town to town;
Our feet were blistered an' weary; our bodies were racked with
pain;
An' some on us fell by the roadside never to rise again.

11

I dreamed I stood on the battle-field with the bullets a whis'lin' by;
With the smoke so thick about me that I couldn't see the sky;
With the cannon around me roarin', like bursts o' thunder sound,
Where the dead an' dyin' together lay in heaps upon the ground.
Where menny a fallen hero, with his faint, expirin' breath,
Ez his gallyant comrades rushed along in the'r last wild charge
    o' death,
Riz up an' cheered 'em forward, from the furrer where he lay
A burnin' with thirst an' fever, while his life-blood ebbed away.
Where the sun went down at the close o' day, with a red an' awful
    glare,
While the terrible cries o' the wounded resounded thro' the air,
Where down in the dark ravines at night, in trenches long an' deep,
We buried our dead an' left 'em to the'r last unbroken sleep.

When the yeller leaves were fallin', in the hospital I lay,
An' tho' we hed won a battle, my heart wus far from gay;
Fur both o' my boys were sleepin' beneath a Southern sod,
By a couple o' Rebel bullets the'r souls were sent to God.
My heart seemed well-nigh broken, but I gloried in the'r fall;
Fur I giv 'em both to my country,— my *pride*, my HOPE, my ALL !
An' oft, in the cold December, when the fields were frozen hard,
On the banks o' the bleak Potomac, I stood in the snow on guard.
I watched the stars above me, an' waited the dawn o' day,
An' longed fur the cheerful firelight o' the old home far away.
Once more o'er hill an' holler, with frozen hands an' feet,
J tramped with my tired companions in that terrible retreat.
We stood by the deep, broad river, a panicky-stricken throng,
With the enemy clost behind us a hundred thousand strong.

"WHERE MENNY A FALLEN HERO, WITH HIS FAINT, EXPIRIN' BREATH,
 EZ HIS GALLYANT COMRADES RUSHED ALONG IN THE'R LAST WILD CHARGE O' DEATH,
 RIZ UP AN' CHEERED 'EM FORWARD, FROM THE FURRER WHERE HE LAY
 A BURNIN' WITH THIRST AN' FEVER, WHILE HIS LIFE-BLOOD EBBED AWAY."

My dream wus changed.   Above me I saw a cloudy sky;
Once more in a *Southern prison* in anguish I seemed to lie,
With nothin' o'erhead fur shelter, on a pile o' moldy hay,
With hundreds around me starvin' an' dyin' day by day.
We were tortured beyond endurance, while Rebel *fiends* stood by,
Who gloated upon our agony an' smiled to see us die.

Hannah, I woke from my awful dream, with the cold sweat on my
        brow,
An' I thank the LORD with all my soul that the War is over now;
That over our country, everywhere, the old flag yet remains;
That the millions are free from bondage who once were held in
        chains.

Under the wavin' Southern pines my fallen comrades sleep,
Down in the darksome trenches, in menny a molderin' heap,
An' beautiful wimmin scatter flowers, on Decoration-Day,
Over the dust o' the BOYS IN BLUE an' the bones o' the boys in
        gray.

DEACON DAY.

THE church hez been an' voted straight, agin my voice an' views,
To put a carpet on the floor an' quishuns in the pews.
I've been a deacon, true an' square, fur twenty years or more,
An' never yet hev seen no need o' carpetin' the floor.

I've helped to build the old church up, an' I hev done my share
To feed its preacher every year an' keep it in repair.
I've took my place each Sabbath day, contented ez could be,
An' I hev alwus found my seat wus soft enough fur me.

I've of'en found myself obleeged to give my boys a shake,
To make 'em mind the preacher's text an' keep 'emselves awake.
But when they get the carpets down an' stuffin' in each pew,
We'll all o' us begin to snore afore the sarmon's through.

The stoves 'll soon be pitched aside, to hev a furniss fire.
They'll vote to hev a vestybule, an' orgin in the choir.
But when they get the'r fixin's in, an' gewgaws on the door,
I'll never feel to home again ez I hev felt afore.

15

FARMER WHITE.

YOU may talk o' the joys o' the farmer,
   An' envy his free, easy life;
You may sit at his bountiful table,
   An' praise his industrious wife.
Ef you chopped in the woods in the winter,
   Or follered the furrer all day •
With a team o' unruly young oxen
   An' feet heavy loaded with clay;
Ef you held the old plow, I'm a thinkin'
   You'd sing in a different way.

You may dream o' the golden-eyed daisies
   An' lilies, that wear sech a charm;
But it gives me a heap o' hard labor
   To keep 'em from sp'ilin' my farm.
You may pictur' the skies in the'r splendor,
   The landscapes so full o' repose,
But I never get time to look at 'em
   Except when it rains or it snows.
You may sing o' the song birds o' summer;
   I'll 'tend to the hawks an' the crows.

You may write o' the beauties o' natur',
   An' dwell on the pleasur's o' toil;
But the good things we hev on our table
   All hev to be dug from the soil;

An' our beautiful, bright, golden butter,
  Perhaps you may never hev larned,
Makes a heap o' hard work fur the wimmin;
  It hez to be cheerfully churned,
An' the cheeses, so plump in our pantry,
  All hev to be lifted an' turned.

"THE STOCK MUST BE WATERED AN' FED."

When I come from the hay-field in summer,
  With stars gleamin' over my head,
When I milk by the light o' my lantern,
  An' wearily crawl into bed.
When I think o' the work o' the morrer,
  An' worry, fur fear it might rain,

When I hear the loud roar o' the thunder,
    An' wife she begins to complain,—
Then it seems ez if life wus a burden,
    With nothin' to hope fur or gain.

But the corn must be planted in springtime,
    The weeds must be kep' from the ground,
While the hay must be cut in the summer,
    The wheat must be cradled an' bound;
Fur we never are out o' employment,
    Except when we lie in the bed;
We must chop all our wood in the winter,
    An' pile it away in the shed.
An' the crops must be taken to market.
    The stock must be watered an' fed.

You may envy the joys o' the farmer,
    Who works like a slave fur his bread,
Or mebbe to pay off a mor'gage
    That hangs like a cloud o'er his head.
You may gaze at his corn-fields an' meaders,
    Nor think o' his wants an' his needs.
You may sit in the shade o' the orchard,
    An' long fur the life that he leads;
But you'd find leetle comfort or pleasur'
    In fightin' the bugs an' the weeds.

PHILANDER COLE.

A RICH old man wus Philander Cole,
  With an iron heart, an' a sordid soul;
  He wus a miserly creatur'.
He would stay to home on the Sabbath day;
The rent o' a pew he wouldn't pay,
  Nor help to support the preacher.

"Bizness wus bizness," he used to say;
"An' people who went in debt *must pay;*
  Or why should they want to borrer?"
He squeezed his victums, he crushed the'r pride,
The widder wept an' the orphan cried,
  But he heeded not the'r sorrer.

What were tears to Philander Cole?
The love fur his money filled his soul,
  An' no matter how he made it.
He only tho't o' the gold he lent,
He only smiled at a big per-cent,
  An' laughed when his victums paid it.

His hair wus white ez the winter's snow;
An', thro' his stingy old soul below,
  A hundred deep schemes were runnin'.

19

His look wus shabby, his clo's wcre mean,
His face wus thin, but his eyes were keen,
      An' the'r gaze wus sharp an' cunnin'.

His tall, white hat, o' a curis style,
Wus enough to make a mourner smile,
      Coz it looked so odd an' funny.
Yet hid from sight, in its queer old crown,
Wus wealth enough fur to buy the town,
      Hed it only been in money.

He carried his notes an' papers there,
An' menny a sound an' solid share
      In railroads, bankin' an' minin'.
An' all o' his neighbors tho't o' that
With great respect fur his old white hat,
      Or ruther its costly linin'.

He lived alone, in a mean abode,
A house remote from the old stage-road,
      In a lonesum situation.
A dozen o' spindlin' popple trees
Jest helped a leetle to break the breeze,
      An' hide it from observation.

The robins returned, with songs o' cheer,
An' the wrens an' swallers built, each year,
      The'r nests in the narrer gables.
To the mossy eave-troughs, rudely hung,
The grizzled old grape vines closely clung
      Like a lot o' stranded cables.

From the cottage roof, decayed an' steep,
The rain ran down to a cistern deep,
    In muggy an' stormy weather;
Where a family o' croakin' frogs,
An' a thousand leetle pollywogs,
    In harmony lived together.

"'BIZNESS WUS BIZNESS,' HE USED TO SAY;
'AN' PEOPLE WHO WENT IN DEBT MUST PAY.'"

But trouble came to Philander Cole,
That tried his temper an' saved his soul —
    Fur "Fortune" hez some strange capers.

While drawin' water, one luckless day,
He dropt his hat, to his great dismay,
    With all o' his precious papers.

Off from his head, like a gleam o' light,
Downward it sank from his anxious sight —
    O ! how his papers did scatter
Amid the sticks an' among the frogs,
Wakin' the wigglers an' pollywogs,
    That wondered what wus the matter.

Ah ! what did those slimy creatur's care
Fur the wealth so widely scattered there,
    Fur they all could live without it.
Soon on the rim o' the old white hat,
A speckled old frog in comfort sat,
    While he croaked to his friends about it.

Philander Cole, with an anxious look,
Fished fur his wealth with a cistern hook,
    'Twus a sorry occupation.
Fur reachin' too far, O ! sad to tell,
He lost his balance an' in he fell,
    With an *awful* imprecation !

A fearful cry, a splash an' a groan,
A gurgle, a shriek, in an awful tone,
    An' no one wus near to save him.
He floundered among the frightened frogs;
He grasped at the slimy sticks an' logs,
    But small wus the help they gave him.

How sweet is life, an' with what strange fear
We come to the close o' our odd career, —
    It puts us to gravely thinkin'.
The drownin' man, with a dyin' clasp,
At the frailest straws will wildly grasp
    To hender himself from sinkin'.

Afore the mind o' Philander Cole
A thousand memories seemed to roll,
    Ez the water settled o'er him;
He tho't o' his useless life o' greed;
O' the orphans wronged, in the'r helpless need,—
    Like a dream all passed afore him.

Up to his chin the water rose;
Then he touched the bottom, *with his toes!*
    With wondrous gratification.
While under his nose were note an' bond,
The wealth o' which he hed been so fond,
    Now what wus its valuation?

It floated around an' seemed to show
The folly o' trustin' to things below,
    Ez the hope o' life wus failin'.
"I will give it all," he cried, "to climb
Out o' this murky an' awful slime"—
    His offer wus unavailin'.

There in the water he shoutin' stood,
Till the sun went down beyond the wood,
    An' he heard the night-birds cryin'.

He saw the gleam o' the fadin' day,
On the clouds above, an' *tried to pray,*
　　　Fur he felt that he wus dyin'.

There is wondrous power in airnest prayer,
Fur souls that struggle in wild despair,
　　　In a hopeless situation.
When all man's efforts cannot prevail,
The HAND FROM HEAVEN can never fail
　　　That fashioned the whole creation.

Within the water the miser stood,
Shoutin' fur help, ez loud ez he could,
　　　With mor'gages floatin' round him;
When, providentially passin' by,
A neighbor harkened an' heard his cry,
　　　An' down in the cistern found him.

He saved the life o' Philander Cole,
An' helped to succor his sinful soul
　　　From a far more fatal disaster;
Fur, from that terrible summer day,
His wealth to the needy he gave away
　　　An' his heart to his HEAVENLY MASTER.

A kindlier look his featur's wore;
His way wus brighter than 'twus afore,
　　　The skies seemed fairer above him.
An', when it wus whispered he wus "dead,"
Menny a sorrerful tear wus shed,
　　　Fur all hed larned to love him.

THE OLD-FASHIONED DOCTOR.

THERE hez been a great change in our practis, I know,
    Sence the day when I took my degree;
There are new-fangled things that hev managed to grow
    Till they've got to be frightful to see.
They declare the old systum hez gone to decay,
    That my formulis all hev been wrong;
An' they hint that I'd better git out o' the way
    That the dosis I give are too strong.

I hev doctored the sick, I hev watched with the ill,
    There are thousands I've physicked an' bled;
Were they livin', to-day, they would brag o' my skill,
    But, I'm sorry to say, they are dead.
Yet I of'en hev cured 'em, an' I would engage,
    That were all to come back from the grave,
They would willin'ly tell you they died o' old age,
    An' not from the dosis I gave.

There are some folks I know, in this fault findin' clime,
    Who will speak o' my skill with a sneer;
Ef I hadn't been round, at a critical time,
    I'm sartin they wouldn't be here.
There hev been many changes, ez sure ez I live,
    Sence the time when I took my degree,
But the weak leetle pills an' the powders they give
    All look mighty onsartin to me.

THE OLD PARSON'S STORY.

THEY say I am "old an' furgetful;"
  My style is ez "slow ez a snail;"
My doctrines are "all out o' fashion;"
  My mind is "beginnin' to fail."
They want a more flowery preacher,
  More full o' furgiveness an' love,
To talk to 'em less about brimstone,
  An' more o' the mansions above.

Fur fifty long years I've been preachin';
  I've studied my old Bible well.
I alwus hev felt it my duty
  To show all the horrors o' hell.
Perhaps I've been wrong in my notions;
  I've follered the scriptur's, I know,
An' never hev knowin'ly broken
  The vows that I took long ago.

I've seen menny trials an' changes,
  I've fought a good fight agin' wrong,
The girls hev all got to be wimmin,
  The boys hev grown manly an' strong.
My honest old deacons hev vanished,
  The'r pure lives hev come to a close,
They sleep in the silent old churchyard,
  Where soon I shall lie in repose.

My flock hez been alwus complainin'
  The church wus not rightly arranged;
They voted to hev a high steeple,
  The gallery hed to be changed;

"THEY SLEEP IN THE SILENT OLD CHURCHYARD,
WHERE SOON I SHALL LIE IN REPOSE."

They built up a fanciful vestry,
  They bought the best orgin in town,
They chopped the old pews into kindlin's,
  An' tumbled the tall pulpit down.

An' now, to my pain an' my sorrer,
  They say, "*the old parson must go;*"
I know I am childish an' feeble,
  My steps are unstiddy an' slow.
They want "a more spirited speaker,"
  I'm told the new deacons hev said,
"To dance round the platform an' holler,
  An' wake up the souls that are dead."

I try to believe that what happens
  Will alwus come out fur the best.
They tell me my labor is "ended,"
  "Tis time I wus takin' a rest."
I've leetle o' comfort or riches,
  (I'm sartin my conscience is clear)
An' when, in the churchyard, I'm sleepin',
  Perhaps they may wish I wus here.

PELEG STOW.

STRONG an' healthy, but alwus slow,
  Large an' lazy wus Peleg Stow:—
      Labor an' he
      Did disagree;
Why he should worry he couldn't see.

The tall, thick weeds in his garden grew,—
His wants were menny, his comforts few;
      Leetle he made,—
      He hed no trade,
An' borrered money he never paid.

While others labored, he calmly slept;
While others hurried, he humbly crept;
      An' he seemed inclined
      To be left behind
In the journey o' life by all his kind.

He hed no manhood, he hed no pride;
His fond wife faded, his childern died;
      An' the whole world said
      They were better dead
Than livin' the pitiful life they led.

Friendless he lived, an' when broken down,
Became a burden upon the town:
　　　He lived in vain,
　　　He died in pain,
An object o' pity an' just disdain.

" LABOR AN' HE
DID DISAGREE."

Yet menny will live in sloth an' ease,
Till out at the elbows an' the knees;
　　　The'r means will spend,
　　　An' in the end,
Will go to the grave without a friend.

SUSIE RAE.

LONG years hev come an' gone, dear Tom,
　　Sence you an' I were boys;
Sence we together went to school
　　An' fussed about our toys.

The old brick school-house yet remains,
　　With whittled seats, its halls
Still bear our badly written names
　　Upon the'r scribbled walls.

The master long hez passed away,—
　　Ah, menny a care hed he;—
No more we laugh at his old tales
　　"With counterfeited glee."

How stern he wus, how fierce his frown,
　　And yet his heart wus kind;
The lessons that I larned from him
　　Hev never left my mind.

I see him yet, a grave old man,
　　With wise an' knowin' look,
Still tightly holdin' in his hand
　　His ferule an' his book.

31

I still kin hear my mother sigh
  O'er muddy clo's, an' rents
Torn in my trowse's, when we played
  At "see-saw" on the fence.

The old white church; the mossy mill
  Beside the waterfall;
The pastur' lot upon the hill;
  The chipmucks in the wall;

The shady bank beside the stream;
  The pebbles on the shore;
All pass before me like a dream,
  An' make me young once more.

My leetle sweetheart, Susie Rae,
  Is now a woman grown.
She hez her share o' earthly care
  An' childern o' her own.

How of'en to her humble home,
  Thro' snowdrifts, deep an' white,
I drew her on my old blue sled,
  An' tho't the load wus light.

You, Tom, were jealous o' me then,
  But that wus long ago,
Our youthful feuds an' enmities
  Hev melted like the snow.

With envious eyes I used to see
   Your clothin' new an' fine,
But what wus your disdain to me,
   When her young heart wus mine.

" I DREW HER ON MY OLD BLUE SLED,
AN' THO'T THE LOAD WUS LIGHT."

I cared not fur the stones you threw,
   When, passin' your abode,
I rode the old white hoss to drink,
   Adown the "old stage-road."

I tho't o' leetle but o' her,
   An' o' her pretty ways;
Fur she wus all the world to me,
   In those bright boyhood days.

The birds sang sweetly in the lane,
    The squirr'ls ran nimbly by;
An' this wide world did not contain
    A happier boy than I.

Alas! 'twus but a boyish dream,
    How soon the old love died.
But oh! how sweet it used to seem,
    To hev her by my side.

"It might hev been;" what tho'ts are these,
    Fur husbands or fur wives.
What leetle sarcumstances form
    An' fashion all our lives.

SWEET IONE.

IF ever in this weary world
   A lovely girl I knew,
Whose eyes were bright ez mornin' light
   Upon the sparklin' dew;
Whose cheeks were like the crimson flush
   Upon a rose full-blown,
Whose heart wus kind ez one could find,
   'Twus sweet Ione.

She hed a pair o' cherry lips,
   That opened to disclose
Two pretty rows o' pearly teeth,
   Beneath her leetle nose.
Ef ever voice wus sweet to hear,
   It wus the tender tone
Oft in my ear breathed low an' clear,
   By sweet Ione.

She hed the fairest leetle hands
   O' eny girl in town,
She hed a slender pair o' feet,
   Beneath her gingham gown,
She looked ez proud ez eny queen
   That ever filled a throne,
Not tall an' slim, but plump an' trim,
   Wus sweet Ione.

She loved to stray thro' woodlands gay,
    An' meaders green an' fair,
Where daisies sweet caressed her feet,
    An' sunbeams kissed her hair.
To her the world wus full o' joy,
    An' sorrer wus unknown.
Her heart wus pure, her faith wus sure:
    Ah, sweet Ione!

Again I dream, I fondly seem
    Her fair young face to see;
Tho' she is faded, old an' gray,
    An' far away from me.
My hopes hev fled, my faith is dead,
    My youthful flame hez flown,
An' yet, at will, I see her still:
    Sweet young Ione.

"SHE LOVED TO STRAY THRO' WOODLANDS GAY."
37

THE OLD GARRET.

WHERE the slender wasps on the winders crawl,
An' the spiders creep on the time-worn wall,

In the dusty attic, I sit an' gaze
At the rusty relics o' bygone days.

Under the rafters, rough an' gray,
When we were childern, we used to play.

Over the rubbish we used to climb,
Sportin' with things o' the olden time.

Clo's that our ancestors used to wear,
Silently hang in the stiflin' air.

Bags o' feathers an' apples dry,
Files o' newspapers long laid by.

Spools an' spindles, in use no more,
Lie on the dusty an' creakin' floor.

Gran'father's old arm chair is here,
The sacred relic o' menny a year.

The coat an' cap that he used to wear;
The battered sword that he used to bear;

38

The faded baldric, once bright an' gay,
He wore so proudly on muster day.

A queer old bunnit that still betrays
The pride o' gran'mother's girlhood days,

With faded feathers, an' ribbons brown,
Lies in a box with a dented crown.

Her old hair trunk an' her broken reel,
Her clock, her loom an' her spinnin' wheel,

All stand in the garret, side by side,
Jest ez she placed 'em afore she died.

Tho'ts o' gran'mother's tender care
Live in my memory, fresh an' fair.

Her toil is over; I linger here,
In the afternoon o' my career,

Dreamin' o' days that hev slipped away,
Under these rafters, rough an' gray;

Where the dust o' time, that will come no more,
Lies thickly over the creakin' floor;

Where the slender wasps on the winders crawl,
An' the spiders creep on the time-worn wall.

40

HOME MEMORIES.

THE OLD FARM-GATE.

THE old farm-gate hangs saggin' down
   On rusty hinges, bent an' brown,
Its latch is gone, an', here an' there,
It shows rude traces o' repair.

That old farm-gate hez seen each year
The blossoms bloom an' disappear;
The bright green leaves o' spring unfold,
An' turn to autumn's red an' gold.

The childern hev upon it clung,
An' in an' out with raptur' swung,
When the'r young hearts were good an' pure,
When hope wus fair an' faith wus sure.

Beside that gate hev lovers true
Told the old story, alwus new,
Hev made the'r vows, hev dreamed o' bliss,
An' sealed each promise with a kiss.

41

That old farm-gate hez opened wide
To welcome home the new-made bride;
When lilacs bloomed, an' locusts fair,
With the'r sweet fragrance filled the air.

That gate, with rusty weight an' chain,
Hez closed upon the solem' train
That bore her lifeless form away,
Upon a dreary autumn day.

The lichens gray an' mosses green
Upon its rottin' posts are seen;
Inishuls, carved with youthful skill
Long years ago, are on it still.

Yet dear to me, above all things,
By reason o' the tho'ts it brings,
Is that old gate, now saggin' down
On rusty hinges bent an' brown.

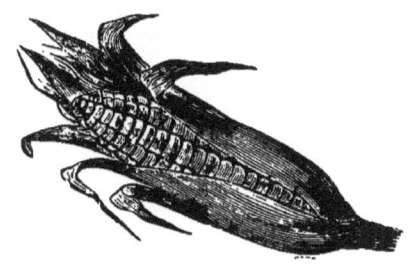

THE OLD STONE MILL.

DOWN at the foot o' the village hill,
   Mossy an' gray, stands the old stone mill;

With its saggin' roof; its rottin' flume;
Its creakin' wheel an' its dusty room.

Groff, the miller, wus old an' gray;
He'd a heart o' flint, an' a surly way;

His eyes were sunken; his nose wus red,
An' the hair like brussles upon his head;

His wrinkled featur's were dark an' grim,
An' he hated the world ez it hated him.

The one bright spot, in his fretful way,
Wus his blue-eyed gran'child, leetle May,

An' a love fur her, sincere an' true,
Wus the only virtu' the old man knew.

The fairest flow'rs, that the world hez known,
In the meanest places hev of'en grown;

The sweetest blossoms, o' all the year,
May soonest wither an' disappear.

The days went by, with the'r work an' care,
The summer roses bloomed fresh an' fair,

An' the winds o' autumn tossed an' whirled
The leaves o' the woodland about the world,

An' the river ran by the old stone mill,
But the gate wus down an' the wheel stood still,

While the village childern sadly said:
"The miller is gone an' the child is dead."

*   *   *   *   *   *

The weepin' willers again are green;
The summer days are once more serene;

Mossy an' gray, stands the old stone mill,
Down at the foot o' the village hill;

But the miller sits in the doorway, there,
With a kinder look than he used to wear;

Fur care an' sorrer hev left the'r trace
In the lines an' wrinkles upon his face;

They hev sof'ened his iron heart an' will,
That were hard ez the stones in his rumblin' mill.

He gently turns, in his pain an' grief,
To his Heavenly Father to find relief.

His wounds seem healed by a blessed balm,
His soul seems filled with a holy calm,

Ez he tells the childern, who come that way,
O' the wondrous beauty o' leetle May.

"THE ONE BRIGHT SPOT, IN HIS FRETFUL WAY,
WUS HIS BLUE-EYED GRAN'CHILD, LEETLE MAY."

GOIN' FUR THE COWS.

THE western sky wus all aglow
    With clouds o' red an' gray:
The crickets in the grassy fields
    Were chirpin' merrily;
When up the lane, an' o'er the hill,
    I saw a maiden roam,
Who went her way at close o' day
    To call the cattle home:

      " Co BOSS, co boss,
        Co BOSS, co boss,
        COME HOME, come home."

The echo o' her charmin' voice
    Resounded thro' the vale;
It lingered on the evenin' air,
    It floated on the gale,
'Twus borne along the mountain side,
    It drifted thro' the glen,
It died away among the hills
    Far from the haunts o' men:

      " Co BOSS, co boss,
        Co BOSS, co boss,
        COME HOME, come home."

Her face wus flushed with hues o' health,
    Her arms an' feet were bare,
She hed a lithe an' active form,
    A wealth o' ebon hair.
Beyond the hills she passed from sight,
    Ez sinks an evenin' star,
Until her voice wus faintly heard
    Still callin' from afar:

      "Co boss, co boss,
        Co boss, co boss,
      Come home, come home."

Soon o'er the grassy knoll appeared
    The cattle, red an' brown,
An' from the pastur' to the lane
    Came quickly trottin' down.
With sparklin' eyes, an' cheeks aglow,
    Returned the maiden gay,
Who waved her arms an' shouted low:
    "Whay boss! whay boss! o whay!"

      "Whay boss! whay boss!
       Whay boss! whay boss!
      O whay! O whay!

THE VILLAGE SEXTON.

THE day is done, the sun is down,
    The dismal night is drawin' near,
Acrost the dark fields, from the town,
    The tollin' bell I hear.

Another soul hez passed away,
    Another heart will beat no more;
The village sexton died to-day,
    His humble life is o'er.

The hands that tolled the bell so long
    Are folded on his lifeless breast;
He soon must lie amid the throng
    He helped to lay at rest.

His hair wus gray, his form wus spare,
    He hed a grave an' solem' mien;
An' mid its menny lines o' care
    No trace o' mirth wus seen.

A rusty suit o' black he wore;
    Each Sabbath morn he used to stand
Behind the ancient entry door,—
    The bell-rope in his hand.

He rang the merry marriage bell,
　To greet with hope the blushin' bride;
He tolled the slow an' solem' knell
　When dearly loved ones died.

" ACROST THE DARK FIELDS, FROM THE TOWN,
THE TOLLIN' BELL I HEAR."

When winter winds blew keen an' shrill,
　When summer roses were in bloom,
He drove the dark hearse o'er the hill
　That bore 'em to the tomb.

4

The bell will toll, he oft' hez tolled,
    An' worldly customs be the same,
An' other hands will heap the mold
    Above his lifeless frame.

We all must die, 'tis vain to weep,
    The proud, the poor alike must fall;
Beneath the sod we soon must sleep,
    The Reaper claims us all!

THE OLD SCHOOL-HOUSE.

I SEE the old red school-house still
    Upon the summit o' the hill,
  In golden sunshine glowin';
I see the shady woodlands near,
The murmurin' brook once more I hear
  Adown the hillside flowin'.

I jine the group o' merry boys
That round the yard with deaf'nin' noise
    An' laughter loud are boundin';
I list'n to the restless din
Amid the whittled desks, within
    The homely schoolroom soundin'.

We stand in line upon the floor,
We read, recite, an' spell once more,—
    Our souls in song seem blended;
Our hearts o'erflow with mirth an' fun,
We grasp our pails an' homeward run,
    When all our tasks are ended.

"How like a bright an' happy dream
The sunny hours o' boyhood seem,"—
    How clear from clouds above us;
How soon to manhood we hev grown,
To fight the way o' life alone,—
    How few we find to love us!

LEETLE JEANNIE.

I.

YEARS hev gone sence blue-eyed Jeannie
 Knelt beside her leetle chair,
An' her rosy face upturnin'
 Lisped her childish prayer.
"Jesus, tender Shepherd, hear. me,
 Bless thy leetle lambs to night;
Thro' the darkness, be thou near me,
 Guard me till the mornin' light."
Never yet wus silence broken,
 By a sound more sweet to hear,
Never words more gently spoken,
 Fell upon my ear.

II.

Once, with joy, she ran to meet me,
 When I went my homeward way,
An' she gayly woke to greet me,
 At the dawn o' day.
Now I hear her voice no longer,
 Softly lispin', sweet an' low,
"Jesus, tender Shepherd, hear me";
 It wus hushed long years ago.
By a leetle marble gravestone,
 Oft' with tearful eyes I stand,
An' I think o' leetle Jeannie,
 In the Better Land.

" SHE GAYLY WOKE TO GREET ME,
AT THE DAWN O' DAY."

YOUR FIRST SWEETHEART.

SHE seemed in your boyhood ez pure an' fair
Ez a snow-flake floatin' a-down the air,
  An' every time you passed her
You hung your head ez you hurried by,
It made you tremble to hev her nigh,
In the tender gaze o' her azure eye
  Your glad young heart beat faster.

Her voice wus musical to your ear,
Her joyous laughter you loved to hear,
  An' while you looked an' lis'ened
You saw her beautiful golden curls,
The envy o' all the other girls,
Her cheeks were red an' the teeth like pearls
  That in her sweet mouth glis'ened.

In the deestrict schoolroom you loved to look
At her fair young face o'er your thumb-worn book,—
  How sweet an' good you tho't her;
When the teacher turned his back awhile
It made you happy to see her smile
Ez you slyly handed acrost the aisle
  The apples you hed brought her.

She said she loved you. You proudly smiled,
An' even fancied, tho' but a child,
   You couldn't live without her;
Few were the words that you shyly said
Ez you drew her home upon your sled;
You ate your supper an' went to bed,
   An' dreamed all night about her.

You, blushin', kissed her ez she went by,
When the girls an' boys played "needle's-eye"
   At Elder Green's "donation";
An' shortly after, upon the stairs,
You saw her flirtin' with Isaac Ayers,
You wished "he'd tend to his own affairs,"
   You felt a sad sensation.

You grew to manhood an' left the town,
She married a farmer an' settled down:
   Your lives were never blended;
You toil'd an' struggled fur wealth an' fame,
An' both o' those worldly blessin's came,
An' after menny a fleetin' flame
   Your youthful romance ended.

You married, at last, a worldly wife,
An' changes came in your busy life
   That left some sober traces;
Your childern clambered about your chair,—
An' weren't you happy to hev 'em there?
No other childern seemed half ez fair,—
   You smiled at the'r glad faces.

Your form is bent an' your hair is gray,
Your leetle sweetheart hez passed away,—
　　'Tis years sence last you parted;
Fur time hez changed you, the years hev fled,
An' t'other day, when you slowly read
In your mornin' paper *she wus dead*,
　　With sad supprise you started.

You dropped your paper upon the floor,
You wandered again by the river's shore,
　　In the midst o' mem'ry's wildwood;
How few there are in this world o' ours
Who marry the love o' the'r boyhood hours!
Yet where in the'r way bloom brighter flowers
　　Than blossoms that bloomed in childhood?

DAYS THAT ARE NO MORE.

WHEN menny years hev rolled away,
 When we no more are young,
When other voices may repeat
 The songs that we hev sung,
When all your youthful beauty fades,
 That Time will not restore,
Some tender tho'ts may come again
 O' days that are no more.

The soul but slumbers to awake
 Alike to joy an' pain;
An' ev'ry holy tho't an' dream
 Are sure to come again.
The youthful heart, untouched by Time,
 Will dream o' days afore,
The old heart lives on memories
 O' days that are no more.

There is a Better Land to come;
 Its gateway is the tomb.—
O! may we meet our loved ones there,
 Beyond the hidden gloom.
How peaceful is the sleep o' Death,
 Fur, thro' his silent door,
The weary woe will never come
 O' days that are No More.

TAKEN AWAY.

TWO limp leetle hands, on an innocent breast,
O'er a heart that is still an' furever at rest;
Two cold leetle feet, that will ne'er go astray,
An' a soul that the angels hev taken away,—
  Taken away, taken away,
  Taken by angels away.

The touch o' your fingers we never may feel,
Nor hear your sweet voice in a plaintive appeal;
Our hearts are a-weary an' dreary to-day:
We long fur the love that is taken away,—
  Taken away, taken away,
  Taken by angels away.

Your bright eyes are closed, we may harken no more
To the sound o' your patterin' feet on the floor,
Nor list' to your laughter, nor watch you at play,
The angels hev taken our darlin' away,—
  Taken away, taken away,
  Taken by angels away.

TWO LEETLE EMPTY STOCKIN'S.

TWO leetle empty stockin's hang
 Behind the kitchen door;
Two leetle pairs o' shoes are thrown
 Upon the farmhouse floor.
The leetle feet, that all day long
 Hev scarcely stopped the'r tread,
Hev pattered up the stairs to rest,
 An' now are snug in bed.

Two leetle pairs o' shoes are thrown
 Upon the attic floor;
The feet that wore 'em, long ago,
 Will never wear 'em more.
One pair o' leetle feet hev gone
 To walk a foreign pave,
The other pair o' leetle feet
 Are quiet in the grave.

60

BUCOLIC BALLADS.

ADONIRAM AND MIRANDA.

I.

BEHIND a range o' wooded hills,
    That hid it from the highway,
A low, old-fashioned farm-house stood,
    Beside a leetle by-way.

With mornin' glories by the door,
    In purple beauty glowin';
An' near at hand, with rush an' roar,
    A mountain torrent flowin'.

Where bobolinks an' robins sang
    The'r glad songs, sweet an' winnin'
While mild Miranda Merriam
    Wus in the kitchen spinnin'.

She hed a han'some head o' hair;
    Her eyes were bright an' jetty;
Her lips were red, her face wus fair,
    Her arms were plump an' pretty.

Her soul wus innocent an' pure,
    Her young heart free from sorrer,
An', singin' like a summer bird,
    She tho't not o' the morrer.

In perfect peace upon the floor,
    The old gray cat wus sleepin';
A lot o' goslin's 'round the door,
    With wistful looks, stood peepin'.

About the old brown barn, near by,
    A flock o' doves wus flyin',
An' in the yard were cacklin' hens
    An' peacocks loudly cryin'.

While round an' round, with whirrin' sound,
    Miranda's wheel wus hummin',
Way down the hill she hoped to see
    Her city lover comin'.

Tho' rustic lovers so't her hand,
    She alwus proudly shunned 'em,
She gazed upon the circlin' hills
    An' longed to live beyond 'em.

How menny look with envious eyes
    Beyond the hills that bound 'em,
How few are ever satisfied
    With fashions that surround 'em.

"WHILE WILD MIRANDA MERRIAM WAS IN THE KITCHEN SPINNIN'."

II.

The sun wus sinkin' in the west,
  The village bells were tollin',
Ez thro' Tom Plumsted's pastur' lot
  A slender youth wus strollin'.

His clo's were o' the latest style,
  An' made without a wrinkle;
What maiden could withstand the smile
  O' Adoniram Skinkle?

Each year he left the city's din,
  To take a long vacation,
An' live upon his country kin
  Fur rustic recreation.

He felt so proud, an' other things
  All seemed so small about him,
He wondered ef this leetle world
  Would long exist without him.

Yet, while his feet with raptur' trod
  The blossoms, bright an' yeller,
O' buttercup an' golden-rod,
  He heard a fearful beller.

Acrost the fields, from hill to hill,
  The frightful noise resounded,
While from a clump o' cedar trees
  A black BULL boldly bounded.

Then Skinkle stopped, with strange supprise,—
    He felt a sudden shiver,
The fond look faded from his eyes,
    His knees began to quiver.

One look behind he quickly cast,—
    O! how the sight did scare him,—
Then down the field he fled ez fast
    Ez his long legs could bear him.

He hollered loudly ez he ran,
    But no one seemed to hear him;
The fence seemed very far away,
    The bull seemed very near him.

Before him roared the mountain stream,
    Behind the bull wus roarin',
An' he wus left to chewse between
    A duckin' or a gorin'.

He stopped in wo', an' all well know
    That t'wus no time fur laughter,
He jumped into the flood below,
    (The bull "came tumblin' after.")

The water dashed an' round him plashed,
    His senses half confoundin',
His hat went dancin' down the glen,
    From rock to rock reboundin'.

5

He swam the stream, he clim' a tree,
    Ere he wus overtaken,
An' on the topmost bough sat he,
    Like one who feels fursaken.

His patent leather boots were sp'iled,
    His slender cane wus shattered,
His dainty wris'bands badly s'iled,
    His clo's with mud were spattered.

Alas! fur him, ef from that limb
    He undertook to travel,
The bull began to shake his horns
    An' fiercely paw the gravel.

III.

The evenin' dew began to fall,
    The stars began to twinkle,
Miranda waited by the wall
    Fur Adoniram Skinkle.

Superbly dressed in all her best,
    She waited there to greet him;
Adown the road, a leetle way,
    She went with hope to meet him.

The dusky bats about the air
    Were round the farm-house flyin',
Her sweet face wore a look o' care.
    She almost felt like cryin'.

An' when above the distant hills,
  The moon wus brightly beamin'
With weary head she went to bed,
  An' soon wus sweetly dreamin'.

While Adoniram Skinkle, still
  His lonely bough adornin',
In clothin' chill, agin' his will,
  Awaited fur the mornin'.

He longed fur wings to fly away
  From his exalted station;
Fur what would sweet Miranda say
  O' his sad situation?

The crickets chirped, the frogs replied,
  The night-birds wailed around him;
All night, with chatterin' teeth, he sighed;
  At morn, Miranda found him.

She drove the furious beast away,
  That watched her luckless lover,
Who dropped to earth, without delay,
  From his high bough above her.

"Alack," sez he, "we only need
  But leetle time to show us
How weak are we, within a tree,
  When there's a bull below us."

SARAH JANE SYLVESTER.

THE evenin' dew wus fallin'.
  Beyond the mountains gray,
The western sky wus glowin'
  In splendor, far away.

The katydids were loudly
  Disputin' in the boughs,
While lots o' jolly bullfrogs
  Were croakin' in the sloughs.

Above, a lonely night-bird
  Wus callin' to its mate,
While Sarah Jane Sylvester
  Stood by the farm-house gate.

She wus a country maiden
  O' nearly seventeen;
Her form wus fat, her featur's
  Were freckled, red an' *green*.

Her hair, a brilliant auburn,
  Wus not inclined to curl;
An' everybody tho't her
  A healthy, han'some girl.

Her ploddin', toil-worn father
Hed airly gone to bed;
A hundred fierce muskeeters
Were hummin' round his head.

"THE EVENIN' DEW WUS FALLIN'. BEYOND THE MOUNTAINS GRAY,
THE WESTERN SKY WUS GLOWIN' IN SPLENDOR, FAR AWAY."

Her simple, lovin' mother
Within the kitchen sat;
She smoked her pipe in silence,
An' poored the purrin' cat.

Oh, sweet an simple girlhood,
  How bright your fancies seem,
When care is but a stranger,
  An' life is like a dream.

When health an' hope are with you,
  When friends are true an' kind,
Afore life's menny follies
  Pervert your simple mind.

While Sarah Jane Sylvester
  Wus gazin' at the stars,
Way down the hill her lover
  Wus clim'in' o'er the bars.

She heard his comin' footfalls,
  An' gin a timid start;
She felt a kind o' flutter,
  Around her happy heart.

His name wus Selah Button;
  A tall young man wus he;
A bashful, honest farmer,
  O' Yankee pedigree.

From his fair dreams at night-time,
  From all his tho'ts o' day,
Sweet Sarah Jane Sylvester
  Wus never far away.

Love cheered him at his labor,
　Upon the stony soil;
Love made his heart more manly,
　An' gin him strength to toil.

O! what delightful greetin's
　That old farm-gate hed seen;
What partin's an' what meetin's
　Both stormy an' serene.

What words o' human comfort
　That old farm-gate hed heard;
What sounds o' love an' anger
　Both solem' an' absurd.

What joyful exclamations;
　What groans o' deep despair;
Fur SEVEN GENERATIONS,
　Hed done the'r sparkin' there.

" I-like-tu-come-here,-Sairey,"
　Sez Selah, with a sigh.
" I-like-tu-hev-yeou-Selah,"
　Sez Sarah in reply.

" Be-yeou-in-airnest-Sairey?
　Or-foolin'-me, perhaps-
Yeou've-been-an'-sed-the-same-thing-
　Tu-them-two-t'other-chaps? "

" I've jest gin one the mitten,
    An' t'other one the sack."
" We'll-sail-life's-sea-tu-gether,"
    Sez Selah with a SMACK!!

Sweet Sarah Jane Sylvester
    In terror sprang away;
She clasped her hands together,
    An' shrieked in wild dismay.

Then Selah so't to soothe her;
    " Don't-holler,-Sairey-Jane,-
I-didn't-mean-tu-kiss-ye,-
    I-never-will-again."

But louder yet she shouted,
    Nor heeded what he said.
From out the bed-room winder
    Her papa popped his head.

An', like a "bull o' Bashan,"
    He bellered, "What's tu pay?"
" Lord knows," sez Selah Button,
    While Sarah swooned away.

He lingered but a minute
    Aside the senseless girl;
His heart wus in a tumult;
    His brain wus in a whirl.

Then from the earth upstartin'
    He turned in mortal fear;
An' down the dusky highway
    Did nimbly disappear.

The sound o' Selah's footfalls
    Hed nearly died away
When, from the farm-house entry,
    Her parents, in dismay,

Came hurryin', both together,
    An' found the'r daughter there,
With her pale face half hidden
    Behind her auburn hair.

Then, kneelin' down aside her,
    The father loudly said:
My! goodness! sakes! alive! Sal,
    What's got intu yer head?"

Then startin' up in terror
    She pulled her boddis down,
An' cried, "A CATERPILLAR
    Hez got intu my gown!

"O MA! TAKE IT AEOUT!! TAKE IT AEOUT!!!"

A SUMMER ROMANCE.

THERE wus a maiden, fair to see,
    Called Cynthiana Cain,
Who loved a young man tenderly,
    Named Ebenezer Paine.

She wus a pretty country girl,
    Ez artless ez a dove;
She met young Ebenezer Paine,
    An' early larned to love.

Yet love is but a transient dream;
    The fancy o' a day;
Its cas'les rise amid the skies,
    To quickly fade away.

An' wimmin' are ez fickle things
    Ez ever hev been born;
While hope itself may take to wings,
    An' leave the heart furlorn.

To that untr'ubled neighborhood
    A city "drummer" came;
An' soon sweet Cynthiana Cain
    Furgot her rustic flame.

The "drummer," ez the days went by,
In female favor grew;
An' Cynthiana Cain fursook
Her old love fur the new;

"SHE WUS A PRETTY COUNTRY GIRL,
EZ ARTLESS EZ A DOVE."

An' scarce a summer day went by
　　But he wus by her side.
He bo't her candy by the pound,
　　An' took her out to ride.

The splendor o' his loud attire
　　An' manners wus complete;
The flamin' necktie that he wore
　　Wus redder than a beet.

On Sunday, in the village church,
　　He looked acrost the aisle,
An' watched each movement that she made
　　With his bewitchin' smile.

She turned her head the other way,
　　Towards Ebenezer Paine,
With an expression on her face
　　O' feminine disdain.

Then honest Ebenezer Paine
　　Grew very lean an' spare;
The "drummer" quickly overturned
　　His cas'les in the air.

Amid the shocks o' standin' corn,
　　In melancholy mind,
All day he worked with look furlorn
　　An' hated wimminkind.

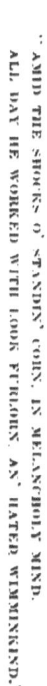

"AMID THE SHOCKS O' STANDIN' CORN, IN MELANCHOLY MIND,
ALL DAY HE WORKED WITH LOOK FURIOUS, AN' HATED WIMMINKIND."

The rivals met, one rainy night,
    The "drummer" talked o' "blood,"
But Ebenezer threw him down,
    An' rolled him in the mud;

Then started fur the Western wilds;
    He could no longer stay
So near the bein' that he loved,
    An' yet so far away.

He went to distant Idaho,
    An' Cynthiana Cain
Ne'er saw his melancholy face,
    Nor heard his voice again.

A sad an' unexpected tale
    Wus bro't to town one day;
When told to Cynthiana Cain
    She fainted quite away.

"The 'drummer' hed a wife at home,
    An' childern, three or four,
An' *twenty sweethearts*, at the least,
    In twenty towns or more."

Afore the cheerless morrer came,
    He secretly hed flown;
An' fickle Cynthiana Cain
    Wus left in tears alone.

HAWKINS AN' ME.

YES, Hawkins an' me run the law in this town,
 When folks can't conclude to agree.
When one's up a stump, an' he wants to get down,
 He calls upon Hawkins or me.

When parties aggrieved go to law fur relief,
 I prosecute — Hawkins defends.
'F'e calls me a scoundrel, I call him a thief!
 But we are the best o' good friends.

The client cares nothin' fur money or time,
 He'll fight jest ez long ez he can;
He'll watch an' he'll wait with a patience sublime
 An' pay all the bills like a man.

He'll sit by the month on a bench in the court;
 (He wants satisfaction, you see)
He finds the seat hard, but he knows there'll be *sport*
 In hearin' from Hawkins an' me.

He'll ha'nt my old offis an' hall like a ghost,
 No matter how much he is bled;
We keep a case flyin' from pillar to post,
 Sometimes till both parties are dead.

Ef you an' your neighbor should get by the ear,
　　An' feel you can never agree,
'Fyou've each got a farm, *unincumbered an' clear*,
　　Jest call upon Hawkins an' me.

"HE'LL WATCH AN' HE'LL WAIT WITH A PATIENCE SUBLIME."

THE WIDDER BUDD.

I'M fifty, I'm fair, an' without a gray hair;
    I feel jest ez young ez a girl.
'F I think o' Zerubabel Lee, I declare
    It sets me all into a whirl.
Last night he wus here, an' I told him to "clear,"—
    An' my! how supprised he did look:
Perhaps I wus rash, but he's after my *cash*,—
    I see thro' his plans like a book.

Some offers I've hed that I cannot call bad.
    There's Deacon Philander Breezee;
I'd sartin said *Yes*, when he wanted a kiss,
    Ef 't'adn't so flustrated me.
It took me so quick that it felt like a kick,—
    I flew all to pieces at once;
Sez I, "You can go,—I'm not wantin' a beau";
    I acted, I know, like a dunce.

Sez he, ez he rose, "I hev come to propose."
    I stopped him afore he began:
Sez I, "You can go, an' see Hepzibah Stow,—
    I won't be tied down to a man."
"Mariar," sez he, "Widder Tompkins an' me
    Can strike up a barg'in, I know;
An', seein' ez we can't decide to agree,
    I guess that I better hed go."

81

He picked up his hat from the chair where it sat,
  An' solem'ly started away;
Sez I, with a look that I'm *sure* he mistook,
  "You're parfec'ly welcome to stay."
My face got ez red ez our old wagon-shed,—
  I tho't fur the land I should melt;
Sez he, "I am done. Good night, leetle one,"
  I *wish* he'd a known how I felt.

To-day, Isaac Beers, with his snickers an' sneers,
  Whose face is ez ugly ez sin,
Drop't in jest to see about buyin' my steers,
  An' tickled the mole on my chin.
Sez I, "You jest quit, I don't like you a bit;
  Your manners are ruther too free.
You'd better behave till Jane's cold in her grave:
  You can't come your sawder on me."

When dear David died (sniff — sniff), ez I sat by his side (sniff —
    sniff),
  He ketched up my hand in his own (sniff — sniff);
He squeezed it awhile (sniff — sniff), an' he sez, with a smile
    (sniff — sniff),
  "You'll soon be a widder alone (sniff — sniff — sniff);
An', when I am gone (sniff — sniff), don't you fuss an' take on
    (sniff — sniff),
  Like old Widder Dorothy Day (sniff — sniff);
Look out fur your tin (sniff — sniff) ef you marry ag'in (sniff —
    sniff),
  Nor throw your affections away (sniff — sniff — sniff)."

My childern hev grown, an' got homes o' the'r own,—
    They're doin' ez well ez they can (wipes her eyes and nose);
An' I'm gettin' sick o' this livin' alone,—
    I wouldn't mind havin' a man.
Fur David hez gone to the mansions above,—
    His body is cold in the ground.
'Fyou know o' a man who would marry fur love,
    Jest find him an' send him around (smiles serenely).

MOSES DOLE.

IN GOSHEN DIALECT.

SAAY straanger, whaare'r ye travelin' tew?
    An' whaat ez yer bizness? haay?
Ef you'll jist hold on I'll ride with yeou,
    Ef yeou're goin' daown my waay.

Iz the ole graay hoss yeou're a drivin' yeour'n?
    Hev yer been in these paarts afore?
Be yeou the feller thet Hiraam Craane
    Seed over ter Oaapen's store?

No? Waal thet's curis. Naow haow did it cum
    Thet yer haappen'd this waay ter steer?
Hev yer straayed awaay from hum ter daay,
    Er got relaashuns here?

So yer doant know naawthin' erbaout these paarts?
    Thet's queer enuff ter kill.
Aint yer never heerd o' Mosis Dole,
    An' ther "Ghost o' Bucklin's Mill?"

The faac' iz, straanger, thet t'other night
    He wuz over ter "Goshen Gaate,"
With a lot o' fellers, a loafin' raound,
    Till it got ter be kind o' laate;

81

"THE FAN' IZ, STRANGER, THET T'OTHER NIGHT, HE WUZ OVER TER 'GOSHEN GAATE,' WITH A LOT O' FELLERS, A LOAFIN' RAOUND, TILL IT GOT TER BE KIND O' LAATE."

An' when he staartid ter traavel hum,
    Twuz mitey daark an' still;
An' he got *sum* scaairt, ez he cum erlong
    Thro' the holler by "Bucklin's Mill."

Ez he hurri'd acrost the old stun bridge,
    In a lively kind o' waay,
The moon cum aout from the big blaack claouds,
    An' the holler lit up like daay.

He whis'led ter keep hiz c'uridge up,
    An' ter show he didn't caare;
When a Injun waar-whoop, laoud an' long,
    Went screechin' erlong the air.

He staartid up, like a fri'ten'd pup,
    An' he pitched rite over a log;
An' the hair on hiz head jist riz rite up,
    Like the brussles on a hog;

Then hop't to hiz feet an' cut an' run
    Like thunder over the hill;
An' tole the naabors o' all he seed,
    In the holler by "Bucklin's Mill."

They loadid the'r rusty muskits up,
    An' caallin' the'r dogs erlong,
Awaay they staartid, ez braave ez bears,
    A couple o' doz'n strong;

But when they got ter the top o' the hill,
   It look't so gloomy b'low,
Ther' waant a feller, in all the'r craowd,
   Could git up hiz pluck ter go.

The dogs beginned ter wurry an' whine,—
   Wy! they wouldn't even staay;
They twistid the'r tails, atween the'r legs,
   An' silently sneaked awaay.

So, the naabors, they putter'd till mornin' cum,
   An' then went daown the hill;
The waater wuz rushin' erlong the fleume,
   But everythin' else wuz still.

An' jist rite over the old stun bridge
   Thaare sot on a big dead tree
A waallopin' great *hoot-aowl* that kep'
   A blinkin' hiz eyes on me.

Hold up yer hoss, I live rite here.
   My naame? Wy, bless yer soul,
Rite over thet hill iz "Bucklin's Mill,"
   An' I am Mosis Dole.

POPPIN' CORN.

'TWUS on a winter evenin',
   The clock hed jest struck nine,
I sot inside the farm-house,
   With Polly Angeline.
The old folks both wus sleepin',
   I heard her snorin' sire,
Ez she an' I wus keepin'
   Awake around the fire;
While up the chimbley leapin'
   The sparks flew higher an' higher.

Now she wus jest the sweetest
   O' all the girls I knew;
An' while I sot aside her,
   The minutes more than flew.
At last to me sez Polly,
   "Ef we stay here till morn,
'Twill make the night more jolly
   To pop a leetle corn."
Sez I, "You're right, I golly!
   Ez sure ez you were born."

I knew that she wus willin',
   I tho't I jest would melt;
I'd gin a bran new shillin'
   To told her how I felt.

The corn wus soon a poppin',
    An' she wus talkin' gay,
My heart it kep' a floppin,
    But nothin' could I say,
The corn it kep' a droppin';
    I wished I wus away.

At last she took the popper
    An' laid it on the floor;
An', redder than a copper,
    She went an' shut the door;
An' then, a minute stoppin',
    She came a leetle nigher,
An' whispered, "Du the poppin',
    An' I will tend the fire."
I felt my heart a hoppin',
    But I wus bound to try her.

Nex' Chris'mus I wus married
    To Polly Angeline;
An' now we pull together,
    With childern eight or nine;
They make a heap o' moppin',
    Altho' our house is small,
An' it jest keeps us hoppin'
    To clothe an' feed 'em all.
An' now I must be stoppin',
    I hear the baby bawl.

THE JOLLY OLD BLACKSMITH.

I'M a jolly old blacksmith, with grizzled hair,
  My face is smutty, I own;
I'm rough an' tough, but I hev'n't a care,
  I'm able to go alone.
Clink, clang, clink, clang, clink, clink, clink,
Plenty to eat an' plenty to drink.
Rough an' tough an' hearty, you see,
Wouldn't you like to live like me?

I'm a merry old blacksmith: I've childern three,
  They're full o' mischief an' fun;
They're cute an' clean, ez babies can be,
  An' bright ez the mornin' sun.
Clink, clang, clink, clang, clink, clink, clink,
Plenty to eat an' plenty to drink;
Rough an' tough an' hearty, you see,
Wouldn't you like to live like me?

I'm a happy old blacksmith, my home is neat;
  I hev no mor'gage to pay.
My house is snug, an' my wife is sweet,
  Her temper is alwus gay
Clink, clang, clink, clang, clink, clink, clink,
Plenty to eat an' plenty to drink;
Rough an' tough an' hearty, you see,
Wouldn't you like to live like me?

"I'M ROUGH AN' TOUGH, BUT I HEV'N'T A CARE."

THE ACHIN' BACK.

IN the corn-field all the day,
    I've dug an' sweat an' hoed away,
My back does ache ez if 'twould break,
    An' sech is the fate o' the farmer, O !
      Sech is the fate o' the farmer.
        The weeds will grow,
        An' he must hoe.
      Sech is the fate o' the farmer.

"IN THE CORN-FIELD ALL THE DAY,
I'VE DUG AN' SWEAT AN' HOED AWAY."

When I see the western sun
Sink out o' sight, my work is done.
My wife complains, nor heeds my pains,
  An' sech is the fate o' the farmer, O !
    Sech is the fate o' the farmer.
      The weeds will grow,
      An' he must hoe,
    Sech is the fate o' the farmer.

An' at last to bed I creep,
An' lie all night, too tired to sleep,
To start, at morn, back to the corn,
  An' sech is the fate o' the farmer, O !
    Sech is the fate o' the farmer.
      The weeds will grow,
      An' he must hoe,
    Sech is the fate o' the farmer.

MY FATHER'S OLD SCARECROW.

MY father's old scarecrow once stood in the corn,
An old-fashioned scarecrow, absurd an' furlorn.
Its legs were but bean poles; its body wus straw;
The wu'st lookin' scarecrow that ever I saw.
    My father's old scarecrow, his old-fashioned scarecrow,
    His ragged old scarecrow, that stood in the corn.

Its featur's were saller; its aspect wus wild;
Its eyes never slumbered; its lips never smiled;
It frightened the hosses, far more than the crows,
That sat on its shoulders an' pecked at its nose.
    My father's old scarecrow, his old-fashioned scarecrow,
    His ragged old scarecrow, that stood in the corn.

My father's old scarecrow hez gone to decay,
A tramp took its trowse's an' wore 'em away.
Yet of'en, in fancy, I see in the corn,
That ragged old scarecrow, absurd an' furlorn.
    My father's old. scarecrow, his old-fashioned scarecrow,
    His ragged old scarecrow, that stood in the corn.

CROWS IN THE CORN.

W AKE up, John!
    An' come an' milk the cows,
The robins an' the bluebirds are a singin' in the boughs,
    The sun hez been in sight
    An hour above the hill,
It's time to feed the hosses an' to give the pigs the'r swill.

JOHN.

Caw, caw, caw,
The crows are in the corn.
Caw, caw, caw,
Get up an' blow your horn!
Caw, caw, caw,
Ske-daw! ske-daw! ske-daw!
Crows are jest the meanest things a body ever saw.

John, come home,
Ez quickly ez you can,
O! drop your hoe an' leave your row, an' bring the hired man.
The cows hev jumped the bars,
An' got into the rye,
The pigs are in the garden, they hev broken from the sty.
Caw, caw, caw,
The crows are in the corn,
Caw, caw, caw,
Get up an' blow your horn!
Caw, caw, caw,
Ske-daw! ske-daw! ske-daw!
Farmin' is the hardest life a body ever saw.

THE SECOND WIFE.

A MELANCHOLY woman lay,
   In sickness, on her bed;
An' in a faint an' broken voice,
   To her sad husband said:
"Dear David, when my earthly form
   Hez turned to lifeless clay,
O! wait an' weep a leetle while,
   Nor throw yourself away.
I know a woman, kind an' true,
   On whom you may depend,—
O! marry Arabella Jones,
   She is my fondest friend."

"Yes, Mollie, I hev much desired
   To talk o' this afore,
Fur Arabella Jones an' I
   Hev tho't the matter o'er."
"Then you an' Arabella Jones
   Hev been *too* smart an' sly,—
I tell you, David Wilkinson,
   I'm not a goin' to die."
Her dark eyes flashed, her strength returned,
   She left her bed o' pain,
A week hed hardly passed away
   When she wus well again.

"GAYLY SING THE SUMMER
SONG BIRDS."—*Page 99.*

SONGS OF NATURE.

BIRD SONG.

THERE'S a choir of happy voices in the woodlands sweetly
    singing;
  Out amid the apple blossoms we can hear them all the day,
And with glad and joyous music all the leafy boughs are ringing.
  Gayly sing the summer song-birds. How we wonder what they say.
      "Twitter, twitter, twiddle, twiddle,"
      Like a flute or like a fiddle;
"Pee-wee, pee-wee, see, see, see me, see me twitter all the day.
      Clinkum, clinkum, bobolinkum,
      Chirk, chirk, chirk, O! whiskodinkum,
Twit, wit, wit, wit, cheer up, cheer up." How we wonder what they
  say.

While we look and while we listen we can see their plumage glisten
  In among the lilac bushes, down amid the tangled grass,—
Perched on hollyhock and thistle, we can watch them while they
  whistle,—
  They go whirling by the window, loudly chirping as they pass.
      "Twitter, twitter, twiddle, twiddle,"
      Like a flute or like a fiddle·

"Pee-wee, pee-wee, see, see, see me, see me twitter all the day.
        Clinkum, clinkum, bobolinkum,
        Chirk, chirk, chirk, O! whiskodinkum,
Twit, wit, wit, wit, cheer up, cheer up." How we wonder what they
    say.

Round and round the farm-house flying, sweetly singing, loudly
    crying,
    Warbling 'mid the trembling tree-tops, we can hear them all the
        day;
While the morning light is breaking, while the drowsy world is
    waking,
    Gayly sing the summer song-birds. How we wonder what they say.
        "Twitter, twitter, twiddle, twiddle,"
        Like a flute or like a fiddle;
"Pee-wee, pee-wee, see, see, see me, see me twitter all the day,
        Clinkum, clinkum, bobolinkum,
        Chirk, chirk, chirk, O! whiskodinkum."
Gayly sing the summer song-birds. How we wonder what they say.

SUMMER IS GONE.

"WE ALL DO FADE AS A LEAF."

SUMMER is gone, and the flowers are dying;
Coldly the clouds 'round the mountain-tops play;
Over the hillsides, the autumn winds sighing,
  Scatter the leaves of the woodland away.
    Withered the lilies lie,—
    Sadly the robins cry,—
    Homeward the swallows fly,—
      Winter is near.

Orphans are crying and widows are weeping,
  Strong men are crushed by their sorrow and care,
Mothers are moaning for little ones sleeping
  Under the willows, now leafless and bare.
    How soon we all grow gray,—
    How fast we pass away,—
    How like the leaves decay,
      Year after year.

101

THE VILLAGE BELLS.

ONCE more, once more, my native shore
In beauty greets my gaze:
Again I walk the cottage floor,
  To dream of bygone days.
The leaves are bright with silver light,
  And through the evening air
Once more I hear the village bells,
  That sound the hour of prayer.
        Tolling, rolling,
        Twanging, clanging,
          At the close of day;
        O'er hill and hollow sounding,
        From rock to rock rebounding,
          Their echoes die away.

O cheerful chimes of better times !
  I'm growing old and gray,
My feet, through other lands and climes,
  Have wandered far away;
I gladly hear your carols clear
  In many a joyous strain;
You come like music to my ear
  To greet me home again.
        Tolling, rolling,
        Twanging, clanging,

At the close of day;
O'er hill and hollow sounding,
From rock to rock rebounding,
Your echoes die away.

THE THUNDERSTORM.

DOWN the mountains darkly creeping,
　　Through the woodlands wildly sweeping,
　The storm bursts on the land.
　　　The rain is pouring,
　　　The wind is loudly roaring
　In tones sublime and grand.
Flashing, crashing, growling, grumbling,
Rumbling, rumbling, rolling, rumbling,
　　　Comes the thunderstorm.

Round and round the birds are flying,
Loudly screaming, sharply crying;
　　They fear the falling rain.
　　　The windows rattle,
　　　The frightened sheep and cattle
　Come leaping down the lane.
Flashing, crashing, growling, grumbling,
Rumbling, rumbling, rolling, rumbling,
　　　Comes the thunderstorm.

Soon the mountain-tops glow brightly,
And the raindrops patter lightly
　　Upon the roof o'erhead;
　　　The sunbeams tender
　　　Break through the clouds in splendor,

The thunderstorm has fled.
Flashing, crashing, growling, grumbling,
Rumbling, rumbling, rolling, rumbling,
Dies the thunderstorm.

"DOWN THE MOUNTAINS DARKLY CREEPING,
THROUGH THE WOODLANDS WILDLY SWEEPING,
THE STORM BURSTS ON THE LAND."

THE MOUNTAIN STREAM.

MURMURING stream,
　　Brightly you beam,
Through the fair valleys you glisten and gleam,
　　From the green hills,
　　From the clear rills,
Turning the wheels of the mossy old mills.
　　Murmuring stream,
　　　　Glide on your way;
　　Glitter and gleam,
　　　　Day after day;
Leap through the vales; laugh in your glee;
Greet the wild gales of the fathomless sea.

　　Patter and prance;
　　Glimmer and glance;
Down through the hollows delightfully dance;
　　Tremble and glow;
　　Ripple and flow;
By the bright banks where the wild willows grow.
　　Murmuring stream,
　　　　Glide on your way;
　　Glitter and gleam,
　　　　Day after day;
Leap through the vales; laugh in your glee;
Greet the wild gales of the fathomless sea.

O! BRIGHTLY BEAM.

I.

ABOVE the hills, the moonbeams glow,
Beyond the fields of shining snow.
The cloudless night is cold and clear,
The leafless woods look dark and drear.
Along the air the sleighbells ring,
While happy voices sweetly sing:
"Oh, brightly beam, with silver light,
The boughs are bare, the world is white,
Beam on, beam on,
From dusk till dawn,
Beam on, O silver moon! beam on."

II.

The evening wind blows soft and low,
Amid the trees the moonbeams glow,
The summer night is warm and clear,
The distant whip-poor-will we hear.
The trembling leaves with beauty gleam,
The starbeams dance upon the stream:
"Oh, brightly shine, with silver light,
The world is green, the hills are bright,
Shine on, shine on,
From dusk till dawn,
Shine on, O silver moon! shine on."

A WINTER SONG.

WE woke in the morning, and found, without warning,
   The meadows and hillsides were white with the snow;
It came all unbidden, the brooklet was hidden
   And hushed in the hollow below.
      Softly, silently, white and fair,
      Floating along through the frosty air,
         Swirling, whirling,
            Shifting, drifting,
      Came the glittering snow.

A poor little robin stood silently bobbin'
   His wee little head in a pitiful way;
The chickens, with wonder, stood solemnly under
   The homely old shed o'er the way.
      Softly, silently, white and fair,
      Floating along through the frosty air,
         Swirling, whirling,
            Shifting, drifting,
      Came the glittering snow.

The north wind was blowing, the cattle were lowing,
   The poor sheep were bleating about the old shed,
The horses were neighing, all seemed to be saying:
   "We want to be sheltered and fed."
      Softly, silently, white and fair,
      Floating along through the frosty air,

Swirling, whirling,
   Shifting, drifting,
  Came the glittering snow.

"SOFTLY, SILENTLY, WHITE AND FAIR.
FLOATING ALONG THROUGH THE FROSTY AIR."

SONG OF THE WOODCHOPPER.

OUT in the bleak, cold woods he stands,
    Swinging his axe with sturdy hands;
Sharply the blue-jays near him call,
Softly the snow-flakes round him fall;
        Gayly he sings,
        As his axe he swings,
    "What care I for the ice or snow,—
    Here away, there away, down you go."

Loud the winds through the tree-tops sigh;
Far the chips from his keen axe fly;
Fiercely the tree-trunks, gray and brown,
Totter, sway, and come tumbling down.
        Gayly he sings,
        As his axe he swings,
    "What care I for the ice or snow,—
    Here away, there away, down you go.

"There's time to work and time to sleep;
There's time to laugh and time to weep;
The chips must fly, the trees must fall
To feed the fire that warms us all."
        Gayly he sings,
        As his axe he swings,
    "What care I for the ice or snow,—
    Here away, there away, down you go."

ROLL, WAVES, ROLL.

I STAND upon the sombre shore, I watch the leaden sky,
I see the storm-clouds coming, and the tall white ships go by;
The sea-gulls on their restless wings are hurrying to and fro,
The waves are wildly beating on the ragged rocks below.

The sky grows dark, the night comes on, the wind begins to roar,
The lightnings flash, the thunders crash along the trembling shore;
The wrecks are beating on the strand, the signal lights I see,—
Heaven! keep my darling from all harm and bring him home to me.

Roll, waves,— roll, waves,— wildly roll away,
Leap along the sandy shore, white with foam and spray;
Blow, winds,— blow, winds,— softly o'er the sea,
Bring my darling home again,— home again to me.

" BLOW. WINDS.— BLOW. WINDS.— SOFTLY O'ER THE SEA,
BRING MY DARLING HOME AGAIN.— HOME AGAIN TO ME."

LAUGHING SONG.

AN IMITATION OF TENNYSON.

I COME from fields of frost and snow,
  My winding way I follow;
I come from where the wild-woods grow,
  I come from hill and hollow;
I foam, I flash, I leap, I dash,
  I glide with music merry
O'er pebbles bright with rainbow light,
  Along the lonely prairie.
    Minne-ha-ha, Minne-ha-ha,
    Laughing, laughing Minne-ha-ha;
    Minne-ha-ha, Minne-ha-ha,
    Ha, ha, ha, ha, ha, ha, ha, ha.

I tremble on the rocky brink,
  My winding way I follow;
I gleam, I pause, I plunge, I sink
  Into the hidden hollow;
I loudly roar along the shore,
  I sparkle and I quiver,
I rush along with laughing song
  To greet the mighty river.
    Minne-ha-ha, Minne-ha-ha,
    Laughing, laughing Minne-ha-ha;
    Minne-ha-ha, Minne-ha-ha,
    Ha, ha, ha, ha, ha, ha, ha, ha.

ALPENA.

I.

RING the bell slowly,—
Humble and holy
Feels every heart, filled with anguish and gloom;
Ring the bell dolefully,
Tearfully, soulfully,
Prayerfully, carefully
Over her tomb.

Brightly the sunbeams were gleaming and glancing,
Gayly the billows were bounding and dancing,
Soft were the winds and delightful the day.
Bearing her throng
Proudly along,
Out from the harbor she went on her way;
Trembling and plashing, she passed from the shore;
Fading from eyes that would greet her no more.

II.

Look at yon clouds through the dark heavens gliding;
See the white foam on the tall billows riding:
Hark to the creak
Of timbers within!
Hear the winds shriek!
O, list to the din
In the air, all around, as she rattles and rolls,
As she breasts the broad waves with her burden of souls.

Must they die ?
How they cry!
Voices in prayer!
Shrieks of despair!
Down in the trough of the sea, with a crash,
She quivers, shivers, and sinks with a plash;
Battered, shattered, scattered, and whirled
Into darkness, out of the world.

III.

Softly the sunshine is gleaming to-day,
Peacefully glide the white ships on their way.
Many are hopefully watching, with sorrow,
Tearfully waiting for loved ones to-morrow.
Dear ones whose voices will gladden the soul
Only where waves of Eternity roll.
Pity the fatherless,
Pity the motherless,
Pity the sisterless,
Pity the brotherless,
Comfort the strong man by sorrow made wild,
Comfort the mother who mourns for her child.

Ring the bell slowly,
Humble and holy
Feels every heart, filled with anguish and gloom;
Ring the bell dolefully,
Tearfully, soulfully,
Prayerfully,
Carefully
Over her tomb.

THE BANKS OF THE MOHAWK.

O DARK rolling river, majestic and free!
You bring back the brightness of boyhood to me
When gayly I wandered along your wild shore,
With one I loved fondly, who loves me no more.
 By the banks of the Mohawk,
  The cataracts roar,
 Where we wandered in childhood
  Along the wild shore.

The song birds have vanished, the summer is o'er,
The roses have faded, that bloomed by her door;
The elms and the maples stand leafless and drear;
The snow-flakes are falling, the winter is here.
 By the banks of the Mohawk,
  The cataracts roar,
 Where we wandered in childhood
  Along the wild shore.

The hopes of her girlhood have flown far away;
Her bright auburn tresses are faded and gray;
Her beauty has vanished; her features, once fair,
Are saddened by sorrow and furrowed by care.
 By the banks of the Mohawk
  The cataracts roar,
 Where we wandered in childhood
  Along the wild shore.

Our childhood is gone; we are drifting to-day,
Like leaves on the river, forever away;
We're leaving the years, and are nearing the shore,
Where storms never beat and no cataracts roar.
  By the·banks of the Mohawk
   The waters may roar
  Forever and ever,
   Along the wild shore.

SOFTLY FROM THE PURPLE CLOUDS.

SOFTLY from the purple clouds,
　　Through the mild and balmy air,
Gleams the golden sunshine down, beautiful and fair.
　　Gently, from an April sky,
　　　　Fall the pearly drops of rain;
Bringing gladness to the ground; bringing spring again.

　　So, within the human heart,
　　　　Through the cheerless clouds of care,
Hope, with heavenly light, looks down, beautiful and fair.
　　Joy and gladness come again;
　　　　From the soul all sorrow flies;
And the darkness disappears, as the winter dies.

"GENTLY. FROM AN APRIL SKY,
FALL THE PEARLY DROPS OF RAIN."

113

SOCIETY SKETCHES.

"A KISS. IN THE DARK."

HE was a gay young bachelor,—
His name was Hiram Greene,
He loved a charming city belle,
Called Amarilla Keene.

He whistled operatic airs,
And he could softly play
Upon the flute and violin,
And *"Parly-voo-frong-say."*

He had the costliest kind of clothes;
He bore a stylish cane;
He wore a brilliant diamond pin,
And massive golden chain.

She danced in silks and satins gay,
At fashionable balls;
And in a glittering *coupe*
She shopped and made her calls.

She swept adown the dusty pave
  With a majestic air,
Amid the gay and brilliant crowd
  That thronged the thoroughfare.

And if some little beggar-girl
  A penny chanced to crave,
It was a piteous sight to see
  The look of scorn she gave.

She loved to talk of *bric-a-brac*
  And decorative art;
She thrummed and hummed the wondrous airs
  Of Chopin and Mozart.

She wore a "Saratoga wave,"
  To hide her scanty hair;
And on a velvet hassock prayed
  Whene'er she knelt in prayer.

She had a pair of poodle-dogs,
  With which she fondly played;
Her purse-proud father dealt in hogs
  Upon the Board of Trade.

What wonder that young Hiram Greene
  Oft' came to her abode?
Her love between the dogs and him
  Was equally bestowed.

On Sundays, when the twinkling stars
  Began to beam above,

He hastened down the Avenue
To call upon his love.

She fondly waited at the door
Till Hiram did appear;
He did not miss a welcome kiss
When no one else was near.

One dark and rainy autumn-night,
When Hiram came to call,
The house was dim,—no cheerful light
Was gleaming in the hall.

He heard a sound upon the stairs
Of footfalls coming down,—
Then in the spacious vestibule,
The rustling of a gown.

And then he thought he stood before
The being he loved best,
And, reaching out his manly arms,
He clasped her to his breast.

"Och! Murther; Augh! *Plaze lit me go!*
PLAZE LIT ME GO! I say;
Ye spalpeen yiz! the loike o' this
I *niver* saw the day!"

The gaslight gleamed within the hall;
It needed but a look
For Hiram Greene to comprehend
That *he had kissed the cook!*

SHADOWS ON THE CURTAIN.

I AM a bachelor merry and gay,
  With nothing to trouble me here.
I have seen at a window, just over the way,
  The changes of many a year;
When the curtain is down, at the close of the day,
  There are shadows that often appear.
Shall I tell you the story? Ah, well! you will find
It is only a tale of the commonest kind.

I was romantic and young,—you may smile,—
A very "Beau Brummell" in manner and style;
My features were ruddy, my teeth were like pearls;
I was handsome, and fond of the beautiful girls,
Till an incident happened I faintly recall:
I loved and I lost, but I lived through it all.

What comfort it was, in those moments of gloom,
As I sat in the shade of my desolate room,
When my labor was done, at the close of the day,
And gazed at that window just over the way,
Where a pair of young lovers, devoted and true,
Had built them a nest, and were hidden from view.
The curtain was down, and nobody could see;
But their "tattle-tale" shadows presented to me
Such pictures of rapture, of joy and delight,
I forgot my own grief at beholding the sight.

II.

I am a bachelor, merry and gay;
  I've toiled and have prospered in trade;
My wishes are heeded, my servants obey;
  My bills are all settled and paid.
There's nothing on earth that I know of to-day
  To trouble or make me afraid.

"I FORGOT MY OWN GRIEF AT BEHOLDING THE SIGHT."

Many months passed away; many changes and cares
I could see, o'er the way, in my neighbors' affairs;
Their kisses grew scanty, their curtain unclean,
And seldom together the lovers were seen.
Then came o'er that curtain new forms of delight,
Like imps in a bottle, that danced in my sight.
Some chidings, low spoken, were brought to my ear,
That I was reluctant and sorry to hear;

And loud cries of children in rage and affright
Were wafted away on the winds of the night.
There were shadows of cares that were novel to me,
That made me rejoice that my spirit was free,
That my life was untrammelled by fetters and bars,
That my peace was unbroken by family jars.

"THEN CAME O'ER THAT CURTAIN NEW FORMS OF DELIGHT."

III.

I am a bachelor, merry and gay,
    With no one to love but myself;
I know I am old, I know I am gray,—
    I've plenty to eat on the shelf.
My nephews and nieces are kindly to-day;
    They love me, and long for my pelf.

The window is down, but my neighbors are there;
The lover is living, without any hair,—

His ringlets have vanished and gone to decay,
For fingers, once loving, have plucked them away;
And his shadowy head, both behind and before,
Is as smooth and as bare as the knob of a door.
The daughters are married, the sons are all grown
The lovers are left in the mansion alone,

"I SEE HER TRIUMPHANT, I HEAR HER COMMAND."

And sounds of contention are brought to my ear,
Discordant, unpleasant, and frightful to hear.
I see her triumphant, I hear her command,
I see him submit at a wave of her hand;
And the sounds that I hear and the sights that I see
Bring comfort, delight and contentment to me,
For the woman I loved is still living to-day,
The wife of my neighbor just over the way.

A RETROSPECT.

SHE lived in a marble mansion,
   On a stylish avenue;
She rode in a handsome carriage,
   And sat in a costly pew;
I dwelt in a dingy office,
   My prospects all looked drear,
For I was a poor law student,
   On seven hundred a year.

I puzzled my brain with "Blackstone,"
   And cheerless "Chitty" I read;
With love and law, commingled,
   I filled my hollow head;
She talked of "Monte Christo,"
   And, when I mentioned "Coke,"
She said she always liked *it*,
   "Because it made no *smoke*."

So she became my "angel,"
   She haunted my working hours,
And, when I wandered in dreamland,
   She strewed my path with flowers.
Then I was hopeful and happy,—
   A glance of her tender eyes,
Or a touch of her tremulous fingers,
   And I was in Paradise.

Her voice was the sweetest music
    That fell upon my ear;
Her hands were small and slender;
    Her skin was soft and clear;
Her teeth were white and pearly,
    And nothing could compare
With the bright and wonderful beauty
    Of her glorious golden hair.

It is only retrospection,
    A dream that has passed away.
Both have grown older and wiser,
    Both are a trifle gray.
Her golden curls have vanished,
    And now she wears, instead,
A *little tuft* that is *yellow*,
    Tied up on her tangled head.

She married her "Monte Christo,"
    In the most romantic style,
And they joggle along, together,
    With neither a joy nor smile,
Nor think of the love and beauty
    Their fancy once made so fair,
Ere romance was household duty,
    And pleasure was earthly care.

"RAGS-NOL-IRON."

A PARODY.

THE eastern sun was rising fast,
As slowly down the street there passed,
With strengthless pace, a man alone,
Who shouted, in a doleful tone,
    " Rags-nol-iron."

His dusky brow was low and square,
O'ergrown with bristling shoe-brush hair.
And, like a broken cow-bell, " rung "
The accents of his time-worn tongue:
    " Rags-nol-iron."

He saw the breakfast fires agleam;
He smelled the kitchen's savory steam;
And, as he slowly shuffled by,
He drew a deep and hungry sigh:
    "Rags-nol-iron."

"Here, shut this gate," an old man said,
As down the street the fellow fled,
But all in vain he faltering cried,
A block away that voice replied
    " Rags-nol-iron."

"Augh, shtop your n'ise," old Bridget screams,
" Ye'll wake me misthress from her dhreams;
The ould cloase all belongs to me.
Whisht now! Arrah be off wid ye
　　　　　　　'Rags nould iron.'

"HIS DUSKY BROW WAS LOW AND SQUARE."

"Tak' 'ar' the dog. O'ill sit 'im on,—
Here Toige!—Ah, faix the man is gone."
The creature made a quick retreat,
His voice was heard far down the street,
　　　　　　"Rags-nol-iron."

All day he wandered up and down
The streets and alleys of the town;
All day the dusty, summer air
Resounded with his plaintive prayer
         "Rags-nol-iron."

At set of sun, the noisy knave
Still staggered down the dusty pave,
And hiccoughed, in a tipsy strain,
The same monotonous refrain:
         "Hic-nrags-nrol-iron."

At dawn of day the man was found
Within the lock-up, snug and sound;
There in the saw-dust, on the floor,
He kept repeating, o'er and o'er,
         "Ragsh-nrol-niron,-
Nragsh-nol-niron."

His shoes were gone, his head was bare,
His garments torn beyond repair,
And, from his upturned, ruby nose,
This wheezing supplication rose,—
         "Tr-r-r-ragsh-n-n-nrol-r-r-riron."

THE WORKMAN'S SONG.

I.

B READ, bread, bread,
　　It is little that I crave;
A shelter wherein to lay my head,
And ground for a common grave.
　　The wolf howls at my door,
　　And my hungry children cry,
While wealth and pride sit side by side
　　In their carriage rolling by.
　　Work, work, work.
　　Oh! give me a spot of soil.
A spade, a hoe, or a scythe to mow,
　　And something for my toil.

II.

　　Bread, bread, bread,
　　Is the cry of wild despair,
Of men who have toiled by the furnace fires,
　　And women who once were fair
　　The cry of beggary comes
　　From the lands beyond the seas,
And millions, worn by toil, must mourn,
　　That a few may live at ease.
　　Work, work, work,
　　Oh! give me a spot of soil.
A spade, a hoe, or a scythe to mow,
　　And something for my toil.

III.

Bread, bread, bread,
A world in its bondage calls,
While robbery bold, creeps uncontrolled,
Through the Nation's stately halls.
There are men of wealth and power,
Who are rotten to the core;
And laws are made the rich to aid,
And to plunder the worthy poor.
Work, work, work.
Oh! give me a spot of soil.
A spade, a hoe, or a scythe to mow,
And something for my toil.

IV.

Bread, bread, bread,
May we find no work at all?
The mills of God may be slow to grind,
, "But they grind exceeding small."
The wheels go round and round:
Their rattle is never still:
And fraud and crime, in Heaven's good time,
Must take their turn in the mill.
Work, work, work.
Oh! give me a spot of soil.
A spade, a hoe, or a scythe to mow,
And something for my toil.

THE DEBATING SOCIETY.

A^N old wooden school-house, worn, battered and brown,
Still stands on a hill, in a New Hampshire town.
Its rafters are rotten, its floor is decayed,
The chinks in its ceiling by children were made;
Its benches are broken, its threshold is worn,
The maps on its walls are discolored and torn;
Its rickety desk, its tall, splint-bottomed chair,
And old-fashioned stove are all out of repair.
Forlorn and forsaken, and left to decay,
It stands on the hill-top, a ruin, to-day.

Here met, long ago, on one evening in seven,
The rustic wise-acres "o' deestrict eleven,"
For social amusement and earnest debate
On questions of freedom, of finance and state.
Here gathered the neighbors, all gayly together,
To talk of the times, of the crops and the weather.
Here came the "old fogies," in coats of dark blue;
The matrons who whispered of things that they knew;
The bashful young boys, with their sleek shining hair;
The bright blushing girls, who they thought were so fair;
And many dark spinsters, forbidding and chill,
Who frowned at "those childern, that wouldn't keep still."

'Twas Saturday night, and the weather was clear;
The sleigh-bells were ringing, delightful to hear;

The moonlight illumined the hollow below,
And glistened and gleamed on the "beautiful snow,"
While floated away, on the cold, frosty air,
The curling white smoke from the farm-houses there.

Before the old school-house, secured in a row,
The horses were pawing and tramping the snow.
A warm fire burned bright in the old-fashioned stove.
The light from the candles gleamed out through the grove.
The school-room was filled with "the pride 'o the place,"
And pleasure was seen on each mirth-beaming face.
Squire Sollit was "chosen to sit in the chair";
He walked to the desk with a dignified air,
And, fixing his eyes on the ceiling o'erhead,
He sat, for a time, thinking what should be said:
Then, placing one hand on his smooth-shaven chin,
He pushed back his chair and arose to begin:
  "A-hem!"
The room had grown still, not a whisper was heard,
All listened to hear his first audible word:
  "A-ha! a-hem!"
He quietly clasped his huge hands on his chest;
He twirled his thick thumbs o'er his black satin vest;
And, wagging his round, shining, comical head,
He drew a long breath and then solemnly said:
  "A-ha! a-hem! Ladies an' Gentlemen an' Feller Citizens,
a-ha! a-hem!"
  A little girl giggled, a staid spinster frowned;
He suddenly stopped, and looked gravely around,
And then, quite confused, without purpose or plan,
He grasped the old desk, with both hands, and began:

"A-ha! a-hem! a-has! I said afore-a-hem! Ladies an' Gentlemen an' Feller Citizens, a-ha! a-hem! we hev come to-gether this
evenin' fur the puppus o', a-ha! a-hem! or ruthur fur the ostensi-
ble puppus o', a-ha! a-hem! suppressin' the press, an' the a-ha!
a-hem! a-hevils o' the press w'ich is becomin' so, a-ha! a-hem!
'pressive.

"A-ha! a-hem, Ladies an' Gentlemen an' Feller Citizens, the
press, an' the a-ha! a-hevils o' the press is *be*-comin' very, a-ha!
a-hem! 'pressive —'pressive to, a-ha! a-hem! you an' 'pressive to,
a-ha! a-hem! me ; an', *there*-fore, 'tis to be *ho*-ped that you will
take the best means o' suppressin' the, a-ha! a-hem! press an' the,
a-ha! a-hevils o' the, a-ha! a-hem! press w'ich is *be*-comin' so, a-ha!
a-hem! 'pressive.

"A-ha! a-hem! Ladies an' Gentlemen an' Feller Citizens,
a-ha ! a-havin' considered the subjec', a-ha! a-havin' giv' you my,
a-ha! a-hull idees o'nt, a-ha! a-havin' showed the *ne*-cessity o' suppressin' the, a-ha! a-hem! press an' the, a-ha! a-hevils o' the, a-ha!
a-hem! press, w'ich is be-comin' so 'pressive, I leave the, a-ha! a-hem!
press an' the a-ha! a-hevils o' the, a-ha! a-hem! press to the debate
o' those app'inted fur the, a-ha! a-hem! puppus.

He drew his silk handkerchief forth from his hat;
He wiped his moist features and downward he sat;
Forgetting his chair had been pushed to the wall,
He sank to the floor with a terrible fall.
The old school-house trembled, from rafter to sill.
Above the old desk, near his overturned seat,
Arose the great soles of his picturesque feet
Like haystacks, that stand on the brow of a hill.
He leaped to his feet, with a scratch on his nose,
And asked, in a quiet but crestfallen way:

"Hez nobody present got nothin' to say?"
Then modestly hushed the applause that arose.

Soon young Peter Plumsted attempted to speak;
His "accents" were low, and exceedingly weak;
He twisted his fingers, he shuffled his feet,
His plain, nervous features "turned red ez a beet,"
He fastened his eyes on a crack in the floor,
He stood in confusion, a minute or more,
With quivering lips, and with shivering knees,
And faltered in fright, "a few feeble idees."

"M-Mr. Chairman, I-I told ou-our folks ef they'd co-come
to-to this me-meetin'- to-to-night th-that I-I would speak to-to this
me-meetin' to-to-night, an' so ou-our folks co-come to this me-
meetin' to-night, an' ez I-I told ou-our folks that I-I would speak
to-to this me-meetin' to-night, I-I am goin' to-to speak to-to this
me-meetin' to night. Ou-our folks is here to-to this meetin' to-
night, an' other fo-folks is here to-to this meetin' to-to-night.
Wh-what I wus goin' to-to say wus, that ou-our folks-a-what I
wa-wanted to say wus that ou-our folks, a-with th-these f-few remarks I-I co-*coincide* with your views."

He might have said more, had not Solomon Creech,
Who stuttered and stammered sometimes in his speech,
Arose with a smile on his "rubicund face,"
And struggled to tell what he thought of the case.

"Mr. P-p-p-p-p-Mr. P-p-p-p-p-Mr. P-p-p-p-p-W-w-w-w-why-Mr.
P-p-p-p-p."

He sank to his seat with a look of dismay,
The words would not come that he wanted to say.

A sturdy young farmer, with coarse tawny hair,
Arose to his feet, with a curious stare,
And, scratching the top of his ponderous head,
He turned to the chairman and earnestly said:

"I doant b'leeve in s'pressin' on the cider-press, coz of I did, what 'ud I du with my appels. Hey? Ef we went to s'pressin' on the cider-press, what 'ud we du fur cider? Ef we didn't hev cider, what 'ud we du fur b'iled cider? Ef we didn't hev b'iled cider, what 'ud we du fur appel sass? Life 'thout appel sass 'ud be

> "Ez like a schooner 'thout a sail;
> Ez like a comet 'thout a tail;
> Ez like a fiddle 'thout a bow,
> Or like a winter 'thout a-a-a snow."

Then old Deacon Barlow, who could not restrain
His thoughts on the subject, arose to explain:

"Neighbor Pettibone, we wa'nt a talkin' on the cider-press, we wus a talkin' on the printin' press."

Then followed a pause of five minutes or more,
Till Israel Hubbard walked out on the floor.
He grasped the lappels of his ancient gray coat:
He soberly cleared his unmusical throat,
And, raising his voice to a high nasal key,
He made a great "pint" that but few failed to see:

"Mis—ter Maw-derater, this ere suppressin' the press, ray-minds me o' the pary-bel o' the ten var-gins, who got an in-vite to a big wed-din' in the scrip-tur's. Five ware wise, an' five ware fu-lish. Five tuk ile an' five tuk no ile. An' the hull ten went an' sot down on a big stun by the bride-groom's door. Bime-by they looked up an' seen the wed-din' a comin', an' the five that tuk ile riz up, lit a match, an' lit the'r lamps ; but the five that tuk no ile did-n't get up, did-n't light a match, an' *did*-n't light the'r lamps: an' then the five that tuk no ile, sez to the five that tuk ile: 'give us o' ile,' but the five that tuk ile, sez to the five that tuk no ile : 'we shell not give thee eny ile, leastwise, we won't hev eny ile fur ourselves.' My Friends, ef we go to suppressin' the printin' press *we* won't hev eny *light* fur ourselves."

Being moved by the spirit, a Quaker, in gray,
With *two tones in his voice*, then proceeded to say:

"Yea, verily brethren; Yea, verily sisters; Yea, verily all an' each o' you, the spirit urgeth an' beseecheth me to say that there is a great deal o' human natur' in mankind, especially the wimmin."

The Quaker sat down, and old Ichabod Pease,
Exclaimed, without rising, "*Them's solid idees.*"
While, back in a corner, a "greenhorn" from "Goshen,"
Cried out to the Chairman, "I second the motion."
Squire Sollit looked puzzled, then frowned at his wife,
And rapped on the desk with his broken jack-knife.

The room was soon silent. The chairman inquired
"Ef nobody else," who was present, desired
"To make a few feeble remarks, or express
Some simple idees a-ha! a-hem a-hon the press"?
A young man arose, on the tips of his toes,
Who, gracefully wiping his aquiline nose,
Began, in a mellow and woman-like tone,
To let the great question at issue alone:

"Mistah Speakah, Sah. I suppose you ah not familyah with ouah ways in Boston, but we ah familyah with youah ways yah. Wat I have seen yah to-night cawys me back to the sunny houhs of childhood, would that I wah but a boy or a girl again. Many yahs ago, I juced to sit on jondah little seat meself, when me little feet could scarcely touch the floah. I was vewy happy then. Am I happy now: pon me honnah, I don't know, but would that I wah but a boy or a girl again. Two little boys juced to attend these meetings togethah, in the sw-eet long ago; the apellation of one was John, the cognomen of the othah was Philandah. Now John was an exceedingly bad little boy, but Philandah (evwybodah loved little Philandah) was a vewy good little boy. Aftah many yahs, those two little boys gwew up to be men. John, as a mattah of coas, made a vewy bad man, and finally got into states'-pwison, foah *stealing hams*, but Philandah, deah little Philandah, is now one of the most influential and wespectable citizens of Boston. Behold him yah; he stands befoah you; that good little boy was meself!"

As soon as Philander had taken his seat,
Theophilus Tomlinson sprang to his feet.
Just home "for vacation" from "old Dartmouth College,"
With mind overflowing with classical knowledge;
He poured forth a flood of grandiloquent prose,
And brought the debate to a glorious close.

"Mr-r-r. Pr-r-resident, sir-r-r, fr-r-rom the immor-r-rtal time when our gl-or-r-rious Pil-gr-r-rim Father-r-rs br-r-rought the star-r-r-spangled banner-r-r to this countr-r-ry, sir-r-r, we have been a p-hatr-r-riotic nation. They pl-anted upon the sacr-r-red soil of Massachusetts, sir-r-r, the fir-r-rst gr-r-reat pr-r-rinciples of lib-er-r-rty, sir-r-r. Who can look upon our-r-r beauteous banner-r-r without emotions of pr-r-ride and p-hatr-r-riotism, sir-r-r? Who can stand beneath its star-r-ry folds without a thr-r-rill of r-r-rapture and delight, sir-r-r? The gr-r-randest sensation of my soul is the inwar-r-d consciousness of being an Amer-r-rican citizen, sir-r-r. I shar-r-re this gl-lor-r-rious feeling with ever-r-ry lover-r-r of lib-er-r-rty, sir-r-r. In union is str-r-rength, in str-r-rength is might, and in might is victor-r-ry, sir-r-r. Let for-r-reign foes who long to kill behold our-r-r banner-r-r and be still. Let them per-r-rmit that incompar-r-rable bir-r-rd, the Amer-r-rican eagle, to per-r-ch for-r-r-ever, undistur-r-rbed, upon the r-r-rock-r-r-ribbed summits of her-r-r native hills. To r-r-rise, to descend, and, like the f-habled Ph-henix, r-r-rise again; to sweep fr-r-rom tor-r-rid gulf to fr-r-rozen sea, to· b-bathe her-r-r br-r-reast within the b-bounding b-billows of the br-r-road Atlantic, and westwar-r-rd, like the star-r-r of empir-r-re, take her-r-r way, until she dips her-r-r wings within the salt spr-r-rays of the p-honder-r-rous Pacific, to soar-r-r, sir-r-r, to soar-r-r, sir-r-r, w-w-why to soar-r-r, sir-r-r, to soar-r-r, sir-r-r, w-w-why, g-g-gentlemen, t-t-to soar-r-r, sir-r-r, t-hill she gets so sor-r-re, sir-r-r, that she is utter-r-rly unable to soar-r-r any mor-r-re, sir-r-r!"

He sank out out of sight, and the Squire, with a sigh,
Said: "A-hem! this ere meetin's adjourned *sin-or-die.*"

*   *   *   *   *

Those simple old farmers have all passed away;
The children, who laughed, are now careworn and gray;
Yet still, on the hill in that New Hampshire town,
The ruined old school-house stands battered and brown.
Forlorn and forsaken, and gone to decay,
The old-fashioned school-room is vacant to-day.

THE YANKEE SCHOOLMASTER.

A CHRISTMAS LEGEND OF "MILLER'S HILL."

—   · —

INSCRIBED

TO THOSE WHO HAVE TAUGHT A COUNTRY SCHOOL, AND HAVE SLEPT IN THE "SPARE BED,"
BY ONE WHO ONCE " BOARDED AROUND. "

THE OLD FARMHOUSE.

O N "Miller's Hill," a farmhouse stood;
A low-eaved structure built of wood;
Whose clapboards, weather-worn and gray,
Were falling into slow decay;
Whose mossy, wooden eave-troughs swung
From rusty irons, rudely hung;
Whose curling shingles, here and there,
Betrayed the need of good repair;
Whose ancient chimney, capped with stone,
With lichens partly overgrown,
Above the sagging roof, looked down
Upon the spires of Brandon town.

An old gray barn was built near by,
With heavy girths and scaffolds high;
With solid sills and massive beams,
And through the cracks and open seams,

The slanting sunshine used to play,
In golden gleams upon the hay;
Where oft, with many a merry shout,
The children jumped and played about
At hide-and-seek, or looked with care
For hidden nests in corners there,
Where oft at morn they used to hear
The cackling hen and chanticleer.

Where, by the broad floor 'neath the mows,
Were cribs and stanchions for the cows,
And strong plank stalls where horses stood,
To eat their hay from racks of wood,
And, in a corner stowed away,
A fanning-mill and old red sleigh,
Where jolly farmboys husked at night
The golden corn by candle-light,
And hung their lanterns by the bay,
On pitchforks thrust into the hay;
Where, sheltered from autumnal rain,
With thundering flails they threshed the grain.

THE SEASONS.

Each year the hum of honey-bees
Was heard amid the apple-trees.
The lilacs bloomed; the locusts fair
With their sweet fragrance filled the air.
The stubble-fields were plowed and sown;
The warm rain fell; the bright sun shone;
The robins sang; the green grass grew;
The roses blossomed in the dew;

"ON 'MILLER'S HILL,' A FARMHOUSE STOOD,
A LOW-EAVED STRUCTURE BUILT OF WOOD."

The tall red hollyhock once more
Bloomed brightly by the farmhouse door;
The sunflower bent its gaudy head;
The cattle in the pastures fed;
The crickets chirped in meadows near;
And sounds were wafted to the ear,
O'er waving fields of tasseled corn,
Of clattering scythe and dinner horn.
The reapers reaped their golden sheaves;
The swallows left the stuccoed eaves;
The apples, in the autumn breeze,
Grew ripe and mellow on the trees;
The leaves were swept about the air;
The fields were brown; the woodlands bare;

The snowflakes fell; the air grew chill;
The sleighbells rang on "Miller's Hill."

THE ARRIVAL.

The winter sky was overcast;
The snow and sleet were falling fast.
'Twas "CHRISTMAS EVE." The air was cool,
The children hurried home from school,
With laughter loud and outcries shrill,
They reached the farmhouse on the hill.
They came across the kitchen floor;
Nor stopped to shut the entry door;
All striving first the news to tell,
Exclaimed, in concert, with a yell:
"The teacher's comin' here to stay;
He's up the road a little way;
He stopped to talk with SUSAN STOW,
And we ran home to let you know."

The mother stopped her spinning-wheel,
And put away her creaking reel,
Swept up the dusty hearth with care,
Rolled down her sleeves and brushed her hair,
Smoothed out her rumpled gingham gown,
And in her rocking-chair sat down.
Then, striving hard to look her best,
She calmly waited for her guest.

Her ruddy, round and fleshy face
Was bordered by a cap of lace.

Her nose was nearly hid from view
By her plump cheeks of healthy hue.
Her eyes were bright; her hair was thin;
She had a heavy double chin;
Her husband's arms, when both embraced,
Could barely circumscribe her waist.

Of all large women, nine in ten
Will fall in love with little men.
And little men — why, none may tell —
Adore large women quite as well.
They woo, they wed; the man through life
Is quite o'ershadowed by the wife.

THE SCHOOLMASTER.

Soon, parting from his rustic flame,
The tardy young schoolmaster came.
His eyes were blue; his features fair;
His chin o'ergrown with downy hair.
Behind his ears, his locks of brown
Were smoothly brushed and plastered down;
His bony limbs were large and long;
His well-trained muscles, firm and strong.
The tall, stout boys, who years before
Had thrown their teachers through the door,
His rod regarded with dismay,
And seldom dared to disobey.
The pride and hope of Hubbardton,
Was tall Lycurgus Littlejohn,
Who had, his fellow-townsmen said,
"A heap o' larnin' in his head."

(Three terms in Middlebury College
Had given him his "heap" of knowledge.)

He often used to sit between
The fair young girls of "sweet sixteen,"
And kindly help them "do their sums."
They brought him fruit and sugar-plums;
They had their youthful hopes and fears;
His words were music in their ears;
Each smile he gave them had a charm;
Each frown would fill them with alarm;
What envious looks at SUSAN STOW,
His favorite scholar, they would throw.

THE FAVORITE SCHOLAR.

Her eyes and hair were dark as night;
Her skin was soft and smooth and white;
Her lips, like cherries ripe and red;
A peach-like bloom her cheeks o'erspread;
What wonder he could not conceal
The glad sweet thrill he used to feel
Through all his palpitating frame,
When to his desk she coyly came
And, looking up with eyes of love,
Like some shy, timid little dove,
Would softly ask him to expound
Some knotty problem she had found,
What being in the world below
Seemed half as sweet as SUSAN STOW?
Her eyes would flash and, in return,
His face would flush and strangely burn;

And, when he tried to calculate
Some long, hard sum upon her slate,
The figures danced before his sight,
Like little goblins, gay and white:

SUSAN STOW.

And, when at night, with cheerful face,
He started for his boarding-place,
What wonder that he came so slow
In walking home with SUSAN STOW?

THE GREETING.

The woman crossed the kitchen floor,
To meet LYCURGUS at the door;
And with a scrutinizing stare,
She said: "Walk in an' take a chair,
An' be to home while you are here.
Come, BUSBY, take his things, my dear."

Forth from his corner, by the fire,
The husband came, at her desire.
His head was bald, save here and there
Stray little tufts of grizzled hair.
His shoulders stooped; his form was thin;
His knees were bent; his toes turned in;
He wore a·long blue flannel frock;
Gray trousers and a satin stock;
A cotton collar, tall and queer,
Was rudely rumpled round each ear;
His face was mild; his smile was bland,
As forth he put his ponderous hand
And said: "I think I see you well.
I hope you'll stay a *leetle* spell.
We're plain folks here, I'd hev you know.
We don't go in fur pride nor show."
Then, after stepping on the cat,
He took the teacher's coat and hat.
He hung them on a rusty nail,
And, picking up his milking pail,
He slowly shuffled out of doors,
And went to do his evening chores.

THE FARMHOUSE KITCHEN.

Close by the firelight's cheerful glare,
LYCURGUS drew the easy chair.
The savory steam of chickens slain,
Came from the black pot on the crane.
The kettle's merry song he heard;
Upon the hearth the gray cat purred;
While, by the chimney-corner snug,
The house-dog dozed upon a rug;
Along the chimney piece of wood,
An idle row of flat-irons stood;
Two candlesticks in bright array,
A pair of snuffers and a tray.
The time-worn clock ticked slowly on;
It struck the hours forever gone:
"Forever gone!" it seemed to say;
"Forever gone"—from day to day,
In its tall case of sombre hue,—
'Twas fifty years since it was new.
Between the windows, small and high,
The looking glass was hung near by.
A brazen bird, with wings outspread,
Perched on the scroll work overhead.
Beneath, a shelf, the common home
Of family Bible, brush and comb.
Above, from iron hooks, were hung
Long frames with apples thickly strung;
And, fixed upon the wall to dry,
Were wreaths of pumpkin kept for pie.

AUNT REBECCA.

Forth from the butt'ry to the fire
Came "Aunt Rebecca McIntire,"
A sallow spinster, somewhat old,
Whose mellow age was seldom told.
Her hair was gray; her nose was thin;
It nearly touched her toothless chin.
Life's weary work and constant care
Had worn a face that once was fair.

Each Sabbath morn, from spring to spring,
Within the choir she used to sing.
In ancient bonnet, cloak and gown,
The oldest relics in the town,
Beside the chorister she stood,
And did the very best she could;
And, while with tuning fork he led,
She marked his movements with her head —
Her nasal voice rose sharp and queer
Above the deep-toned viol near.

She took the black pot from the crane;
Removed the kettle from the chain;
And made the tea and chicken broth;
Drew out the table; spread the cloth;
Then, from the cupboard, bright and new,
Brought the best china, edged with blue.

SUPPER.

The chores were done; the feast was spread;
All took their seats, and grace was said.
They ate the savory chicken stew
So juicy and so well cooked through.
Before them rich, round dumplings swam
On steaming plates, with cold boiled ham;
With feathery biscuit, warm and light;
With currant jam and honey white,
And, crowning all, a good supply
Of yellow, mealy pumpkin pie.

THE CHILDREN'S BEDTIME.

The supper done, the father took
From off its shelf the sacred book,
And read of Him who stilled the sea
One stormy night in Galilee.
Then kneeling down before his chair,
He asked the Heavenly Shepherd's care.

Soon from the group, with drowsy heads,
The children started for their beds,
Took off the little shoes they wore,
And left them on the kitchen floor.
Upon the wall, with cheeks aglow,
They hung their stockings in a row:
Then, bidding all a fond "good night,"
With pattering feet, they passed from sight.

Dear little feet; how soon they stray
From the old farmhouse, far away.
How soon they leave the family fold,
To walk the shining streets of gold,
Where every hope is real and sure,
Where every heart is kind and pure,
Where every dream is bright and fair;—
O! may we meet our loved ones there.

AROUND THE FIRESIDE.

The farmer left his cozy seat,
With clattering slippers on his feet,
Went to the cellar, where he drew
A mug of cider, sweet and new,
And, from his broad bins, brought the best
And ripest apples for his guest.
Then, by the warm fire's ruddy light,
They lingered until late at night,
Strange legends told, and tales that made
Them all feel anxious and afraid.

AUNT REBECCA RETIRES.

But "AUNT REBECCA" watched in vain
The curling smoke above the crane.
She nodded, dozed, began to snore;
She dropped her knitting on the floor,
Awoke! her eyelids heavier grew;
Arose, and silently withdrew.

Along the creaking stairs she crept,
To the lone chamber where she slept,

And close the window curtains drew,
To screen herself from outward view;
She stopped the keyhole of the door,
She set the candle on the floor,
Looked 'neath the valance, half afraid
To find a man in ambuscade:
Then, sitting down aside with care
She laid her garments on a chair,
Slipped on her ghostly robe of white,
Took off her shoes, blew out the light;
Then, in the darkness, from her head
Removed her wig and went to bed;
Curled up with chilly sobs and sighs,
And, shivering, shut her drowsy eyes.

Poor single souls who sleep alone!
The night wind hath a dismal tone
To your lone ears — you start with fear
At every midnight sound you hear.
When, late at night, with weary heads,
You creep into your lonely beds.
The nights seem long; your lips turn blue,
Your feet grow cold — you know they do.

A DREAM OF GIRLHOOD.

She slept at last, she heard once more
The murmuring waves upon the shore,
Again she sat upon the strand,
And some one clasped her fair young hand
And words were whispered in her ear
That long ago she loved to hear;

And starting up she cried in glee:
"I knew you would come back to me."

She woke,—alas! no love was there;
Her thin hands clasped the vacant air;
'Twas but a dream, she lived alone;
Without, she heard the night wind moan;
While on the window panes the snow
Was wildly beating. From below
The smothered sound of voices came,
Where still with Busby's social dame
Their guest sat by the fading fire,
And watched its fleeting flame expire.
Awhile she listened, but no word
They uttered could be clearly heard.
But soon a recollection came
That sent a shudder through her frame;

The *sausage* to be fried at morn,
The breakfast table to adorn,
Was in the bed-room where their guest
Would soon betake himself to rest.
The clock struck ten—she softly said:
"*I'll get it ere he goes to bed.*"

THE SPARE BED.

The spare bed stood within a room
As chill and humid as a tomb;
'Twas never aired; 'twas seldom swept:
In its damp corners spiders crept;

They built their bridges through the air,
And no rude broom disturbed them there.
The rain, that fell on roof decayed,
Dripped thro' the chinks that time had made,
And on the white-washed walls ran down
In wondrous frescoes, tinged with brown.
The window-panes, with frost o'erspread,
Were warmer than that icy bed.
Cold was the matting on the floor.
Cold blew the breeze beneath the door.
Cold were the straight-backed chairs of wood.
Cold was the oaken stand that stood
On spindling legs that looked as chill
As lone, bare pines on some bleak hill.
High rose that bed o'er things below
Like some tall iceberg capped with snow.
Here every highly honored guest,
When bed-time came, retired to "*rest.*"

Within its large and moldy press,
Hung Mrs. Busby's best silk dress,
Her Sunday bonnet, shoes and shawl,
On rusty nails against the wall,
By Mr. Busby's suit of blue
That at his wedding had been new.
Here, on a peg, his best cravat
Reposed within his old fur hat;
Here, shut from sight of human eyes,
Were rows of mince and apple pies;
With rolls of sausage and head-cheese,
Stored on the shelves and left to freeze.

ENTRAPPED.

From out her cot the maiden crept,
Slipped on her shoes and softly stepped
Along the hall and through the gloom,
Until she reached the chilly room.
Unseen, she crossed the icy floor,
Unheard, unlocked the closet door,
Snatched from the shelf, in her firm hold,
A bag of sausage, stiff and cold,
Then, turning quickly, sought to beat
A sudden, safe and sure retreat.
Too late! a light gleamed on the wall,
And sounds of footfalls filled the hall;
Then to the room came boldly on
The stalwart form of LITTLEJOHN.
She backward stepped and stood aghast!
Then shut the door and held it fast.

With chattering teeth and trembling frame,
Across the floor LYCURGUS came.
He placed the candle in his hand
Upon the spindling oaken stand,
Then closed the door, and, with a frown,
Within a cold chair settled down.
He threw his boots upon the floor,
And, rising, tried the closet door;
But AUNT REBECCA, in a fright,
Clung to the latch with all her might.
To look within LYCURGUS failed;
He turned away and thought it nailed.

Then pulling down the snowy spread,
He put his warm brick in the bed,
Took off his clothes and slipped between
The sheets of ice, so white and clean,
Blew out the light, and with a sneeze
Close to his chin he brought his knees;
Beneath the clothes he drew his nose,
And tried in vain to find repose.
While AUNT REBECCA from the wall
Took down the Sunday gown and shawl;
She wrapped them round her freezing form,
And *blushed* to keep her visage warm.

SUSPENSE.

, The paper curtains, loosely hung
Upon the windows, rustling swung,
While through each quivering, narrow frame
Of frosty panes a dim light came
That made the furniture appear
Like dusky phantoms crouching near.
LYCURGUS listened to the storm,
And hugged his brick to keep him warm.
But colder grew the humid bed;
The clothes congealed about his head;
To feel at ease in vain he tried;
He tossed and turned from side to side;
Each time he moved, beneath his weight
The bedstead creaked like some farm-gate;
His brick grew cold; he could not sleep;
A strange sensation seemed to creep

Upon him, while across the floor
He closely watched the closet door.

AN APPARITION.

Was he but dreaming? No! his eyes
Beheld with wonder and surprise
What man had never seen before,—
There was a movement at the door.
It slowly turned, and to his sight
Came through the dim, uncertain light
A hideous hand, that in its clasp
Some awful object seemed to grasp.
A crouching form, with frightful head,
Seemed slowly coming toward the bed.
He heard the rusty hinges creak;
He could not stir; he could not speak;
He could not turn his head away;
He shut his eyes and tried to pray.
Upon his brow of pallid hue
The cold sweat stood, like drops of dew.
At last he shrieked, aloud and shrill,—
The door swung back and all was still.
That midnight cry from room to room
Resounded loudly through the gloom;
The farmer and his wife, at rest
Within their warm and cozy nest,
Awoke and sprang, in strange attire,
Forth from their bed, loud shouting "*fire!*"
But finding neither smoke nor flame,
Soon stumbling up the stairs they came,

In cotton bed-quilts quaintly dressed.
They heard a deep groan from their guest;
And full of wonder and affright,
Pushed in the door and struck a light.

Deep down within the feather bed
LYCURGUS had withdrawn his head,
And out of sight lay quaking there,
With throbbing heart and bristling hair.
They questioned him, but he was still;
He shook as if he had a chill;
The courage was completely gone
From tall LYCURGUS LITTLEJOHN.

THE DENOUEMENT.

What human language can express
The modest maiden's dire distress,
While standing still behind her screen,
A sad spectator of the scene?
What pen or pencil can portray
Her mute despair and deep dismay?
Awhile she stood, and through the door
She peeped across the bedroom floor.
The way was clear, and like a vise,
She grasped the sausage cold as ice,
Sprang from the closet, and from sight
She glided, like a gleam of light;
Away, without a look or word,
She flew like an affrighted bird,—
Without one moment of delay
The mystery cleared itself away.

CONCLUSION.

Again the snow gleams on the ground,
Again the sleigh-bells gayly sound,
Again on "Miller's Hill" we hear
The shouts of children loud and clear.
But in the barn is heard no more
The flapping flail upon the floor.
The house is down, its inmates gone,
And tall LYCURGUS LITTLEJOHN
Is now an old man, worn with care,
With stooping form and silver hair.
He married dark-eyed SUSAN STOW,
And they were happy years ago.
When in the merry winter time
Their children's children round him climb
He tells them of his fearful fright
On that far-distant winter night;
And after they are put to bed,
When by the fire, with nodding head,
He sits and sinks to slumber deep,
And quakes and shivers in his sleep,
Alas! he is but dreaming still
Of that spare bed on "Miller's Hill."